his other secret

(a stella fall psychological suspense thriller—book 3)

ava strong

Ava Strong

Debut author Ava Strong is author of the REMI LAURENT mystery series, comprising three books (and counting); of the ILSE BECK mystery series, comprising four books (and counting); and of the STELLA FALL psychological suspense thriller series, comprising four books (and counting).

An avid reader and lifelong fan of the mystery and thriller genres, Ava loves to hear from you, so please feel free to visit www.avastrongauthor.com to learn more and stay in touch.

ISBN: 978-1-0943-9312-4

BOOKS BY AVA STRONG

REMI LAURENT FBI SUSPENSE THRILLER
THE DEATH CODE (Book #1)
THE MURDER CODE (Book #2)
THE MALICE CODE (Book #3)

ILSE BECK FBI SUSPENSE THRILLER
NOT LIKE US (Book #1)
NOT LIKE HE SEEMED (Book #2)
NOT LIKE YESTERDAY (Book #3)
NOT LIKE THIS (Book #4)

STELLA FALL PSYCHOLOGICAL SUSPENSE THRILLER
HIS OTHER WIFE (Book #1)
HIS OTHER LIE (Book #2)
HIS OTHER SECRET (Book #3)
HIS OTHER MISTRESS (Book #4)

CHAPTER ONE

Today, I am here to ask about the past, Stella Fall thought, determined.

Stella Fall slowed the rental car. Beyond the ragged belt of trees, the horizon stretched ahead, bleak and bare. Even in the rainy season, a pall of dust seemed to hang in the air.

Home.

It was like being back in her nightmares. She had the same feeling of nameless dread, the curdling of fear in her belly that made her want to turn around and accelerate away.

There was the landmark: the dry, jagged thorn tree that she'd hoped was dead but which remained stubbornly rooted in the sandy soil. Stella had always thought its crooked branches were like clawed hands.

She shuddered, looking away as she jolted down the sand track that ran for two rutted, eroded miles.

Just a few days ago, while tackling the contents of old storage boxes, she'd discovered a letter from her father, who had disappeared without a trace when she was ten years old. Her mother had told her emphatically she'd believed him to be dead. Devastated by the loss of the quiet, kind man who'd been her mentor and protector, Stella had eventually accepted this could be the only explanation.

Reading the letter's postmark, Stella had been shocked to see that the brief, curt note had been posted weeks after his disappearance. Her mother had known he was still alive! She'd never breathed a word about this to Stella.

Now, she was going to confront her and demand an answer. Where was her father? Why had Rhonda Fall lied?

She gritted her teeth as the small car bounced into a massive pothole. She'd lost focus for a moment, her gaze straying to the skyline. She had to brace herself; there was no room for dreaming about the future in the harsh life that she'd endured in the small, clapboard house at the end of this road.

There was the house. Its squat, low outline seemed to cling to the unforgiving landscape.

Rhonda's ancient truck, its rear window patterned with dust, was parked under the scanty shade of an old cottonwood. Stella remembered the school runs she'd endured in that car, with Rhonda either screaming at Stella or riding in smoldering silence, depending on her mood.

Cold fear nestled inside her as she stopped the car and climbed out. She did her best to banish it. What she needed now was resolve.

She raked her fingers through her dark hair, pushing it away from her face. She'd forgotten how the relentless wind always blew it into her eyes.

Reaching back into the car, she took out the carrier bag. She'd made a brief stop in town to make the purchases. Then she walked up the broken path, staring down at the fragments of paving that still remained from the time her father had made it. Time and wear had taken their toll. The stones were all but gone.

But where was he?

Stella breathed in deeply. Then she knocked on the door. There was silence for a few beats that felt as if it was stretching into eternity. From behind the house somewhere, she heard the frantic clucking of chickens.

And then, from inside, her mother's voice, filled with taunting amusement.

"You're late. And you don't need to knock. Why are you knocking?"

Stella opened the door. Hinges wailed as she stepped in, breathing in the smells she remembered. Parched boards, dusty glass, the bitter reek of the wood stain her mother used. The only home improvements that Rhonda did every year were to treat the worn, south-facing outer boards, and how Stella hated that smell. Just as she hated the faint undertones of egg, oil, and cooked cabbage that seemed to linger forever in the kitchen.

She picked up the low-key babble of television as she trod through the tiny hall, barely large enough for the discarded shoes and umbrellas that were piled there, and into the lounge.

Rhonda was seated in her wooden rocking chair by the window.

"Well, hello," she said, turning to Stella.

A rush of emotion filled her, overwhelming in its intensity as she gazed at her mother's slender face, her beaky nose, those bright, intense eyes. Her coarse, dark hair, now threaded with gray, was pulled back into a tight braid. The lines on her forehead and her cheeks were deeper and harsher than the last time she'd seen them.

She stared into the ice-blue eyes that she had inherited. It dismayed her how strong her mother's genes clearly were, and how alike they were in coloring, height, and their slim, lean build. Sometimes, Stella felt frantic that there were other similarities between them. Would she end up the same as her mother? When would the terrible rages, the mood swings, the bitter abuse begin?

Why had Rhonda become this way? Were her mother's mental problems, and her stubbornness in refusing to seek help for them, hereditary?

Every day, she felt like she needed to fight against the threat of the genetic time-bomb that might be lurking inside her. But now, Rhonda was in a gentle mood, a fact that made her deeply suspicious.

"Sorry I'm late. My flight was delayed." Her first words were an apology. How typical.

"It's been a very long time since my only child has visited," Rhonda said softly. "It must be more than two years since I last saw you. How I've missed you. Are you staying overnight? You didn't say."

Stella struggled not to be drawn into the game she knew her mother would play.

"I've been really busy. I've sent money when I can," she said shortly. "I can't stay overnight. I'm flying back this evening as I'm moving houses tomorrow. But I brought you a gift."

"That's very kind of you. Very kind. You have such a good heart," Rhonda murmured, taking the bag.

More than anything, Stella hated the uncertainty about coming home. Would her mother be in outright aggressive mode, shouting and screaming? Or would she be like this – quiet and polite, luring Stella into believing that everything might be okay between them, if she could only try just a little harder?

This mood was worse. It was like waiting for a storm, because she could tip into fury at any moment. The dread of triggering her hung over every word. But also, her mother was more manipulative in this mood. In a rage, she might be more likely to scream out the truth – and the truth was what Stella was desperate to find.

From the knowing, yet guarded expression in her mother's eyes, Stella had a horrible feeling she might already know why her daughter was here. Rhonda was far from stupid. That was another thing she'd passed onto her daughter – her sharp, perceptive intelligence.

"Are you going to open it?" Stella asked, glancing at the bag, hoping that the gift might set their meeting on a cordial footing.

"Open it? Yes, of course, I can do that."

She dipped a slim-fingered hand into the bag.

"Butterscotch cookies. My favorite." She paused. "At least, they were. My physician has said I must cut down on sugar. But don't worry, I have friends who will love them."

Stella gritted her teeth.

"Hand cream. Now that's useful. Pomegranate? How interesting. I can't say I have ever thought pomegranates had a fragrance I would want on my skin. But we will see, won't we? I look forward to finding out." She gave Stella a conspiratorial smile. "And books. I can't wait to read all three of those. With money so short, buying books is a luxury I haven't allowed myself lately. I've had to rely on our local library, which as you know, is not well run."

Having managed, subtly or otherwise, to make Stella feel bad about every single item in the gift bag, Rhonda put it aside. Then she stared at Stella challengingly.

"So, why the sudden decision to make this lightning trip?" she asked.

The chit-chat, such as it was, was over, and there was no point in drawing out the social niceties. It was time to unleash the real purpose for her visit.

"I came to ask you about this letter," Stella said. She produced it from her purse.

Her mother gave nothing away as she saw it. Not as much as a narrowing of her eyes or a twitch of her face indicated that she was aware of its significance at all.

"What about it?" she asked, in tones only mildly interested.

"I must have packed it up by mistake, when I moved my things out. I found it yesterday. It was at the bottom of a drawer. It's from Dad."

Even though she was trying as hard as she could to maintain the same levels of icy control as her mother, Stella felt her voice shake.

"A letter from your father? You've come here to ask me about that?" Genuine puzzlement suffused Rhonda's voice.

"Look at the postmark," Stella said. She kept a firm grip on the page. She knew that in a flash, Rhonda's mood could turn. She could snatch the letter away and destroy it. Stella wasn't going to let that happen.

"Yes." Rhonda peered down. "One of his last letters. It must have been only a month or two later that he disappeared."

Stella felt anger so strong it threatened to break through the control she'd promised herself she would keep, no matter what.

"He disappeared exactly seven weeks before that letter was written," she insisted. "I remember the exact date he didn't come home. And there was also a missing person report filed. You insisted on waiting a full day before you did it. It felt like a hundred lifetimes," Stella said, remembering her agonies as the long night, and then the endless day, had worn on.

Only in the evening had Rhonda climbed into her truck and, leaving Stella behind despite her tearful pleas, driven the fifteen-mile ride to the local police station where Detective Fall had worked, to report him missing.

Ever since then, Stella had suffered agonies of worry over what had happened to him. She'd tried to persuade herself over and over again that her father must have died, but she'd never been able to suppress the powerful, though irrational, feeling that he was still alive.

"I waited because I was hoping he would return," Rhonda told her sternly before returning her attention to the letter. "This was sent from – where?" She peered down at it and Stella could see nothing in her eyes but an earnest desire to find the truth. "Your thumb's over that part. Move your thumb."

Keeping a tight hold on the page, Stella moved her thumb.

Rhonda sighed as if everything was clear.

"Sent from Colorado. Of course."

"What's of course about it?" Anxiety tightened in her belly.

"He used to go to Colorado regularly. Being a neighboring state to Kansas, there were a lot of cross-border crimes the police cooperated on. You wouldn't know any of this because you thought all we did was fight." Now there was a hint of acid in Rhonda's words. "You thought you were your father's little princess and his saving grace. You did not understand that we had a functional and happy marriage. Given that, I can't understand why you ended up so damaged, and so very vindictive toward me. They say only scarred people go into psychology. Would you say that's true? Has it guided your career choice?" She stared critically at Stella.

She was about to spit back an angry reply before she realized her mother was deliberately baiting her into losing her temper. Plus, she was skillfully changing the subject.

Stella dug her nails into her palm as hard as she could, glad of the distraction that the stabbing pain provided. At least it helped her keep her focus as her mother continued.

"That's exactly why I guided you away from that path. You're an unstable person, Stella. You can't cope with the stresses of a career, particularly not in law enforcement. That's why I always advised you against it. If you want wealth, and a more comfortable life than I had, then marry well. Choose someone better than I did."

Stella wasn't going to take the bait. She was not going to walk into the trap of discussing her Master's degree in forensic psychology, and her recent decision to join the FBI. Her mother did not need to know that. She didn't dare to share the triumphs of her graduation from one of the toughest law enforcement training programs, nor her job offer to join the team in the FBI New Haven field office. In fact, that was the reason why this was such a short visit. She had needed to speak to her mother in person, but today was the only day she'd had to spare, with moving into her brand new apartment in New Haven, and starting her new job on Tuesday.

Stella knew her mother would twist and corrupt her achievements and make her feel ashamed of herself. She'd done it time and time again. It was better to say nothing.

Instead, Stella forced herself to ignore the noise and distractions and focused on the purpose of her visit. Rhonda was remaining calm, which in itself was a huge red flag. Stella had to push on. She had to! There really must be something hidden.

"The postmark," she insisted.

Rhonda shrugged. "In the backwaters of Colorado, they cleared mail when they felt like it. Your father and I used to laugh about it. Most times, he'd get back before his letters."

Stella felt herself weaken. This sounded plausible. It could actually be.

But then she remembered her mother's talent for deceiving her. Stubbornly, she stuck to her version.

"Seven weeks? I think that's pushing it. From the local postbox to the post office, it would be a few days at most. Even in backwaters, the US Mail worked. Especially in backwaters," Stella argued further.

"And why did he say in the letter that you should tell me when I was ready? What did he mean? Can you explain that?" she challenged.

Rhonda looked furious for a moment, as if Stella had caught her out. Then she shook her head sadly. "My precious girl, you are hell bent on tormenting yourself with this, aren't you?"

Her voice was soft, but her gaze lanced Stella like a steel blade.

"Why do you say that?" Now Stella wished her mother would tip over into anger. This relentless calm was a barrier she couldn't break through.

"You won't like the truth," Rhonda's voice dropped to a whisper.

"Maybe. But I want it. I deserve it."

Stella struggled to keep her voice indifferent, casual, even. Meanwhile, her heart was pounding so loudly that blood was roaring in her ears. Finally, her mother was going to relent. She was going to tell her what had really happened. Could she sense how keyed up she was? It would be better if Rhonda didn't realize that. If she thought Stella didn't care too much, she would be more willing to tell her everything.

"The truth," Rhonda whispered.

"Please," Stella said quietly.

"Alright then. I will."

Stella leaned closer. Finally, she was going to get the answers she craved.

And then, Rhonda flung her head back and screamed out the words.

"There are no answers! There is only one reality, that your father abandoned us. He turned his back on his family. On you, his only child, who hero-worshiped him even though he was scum. He walked away. He hated us! Hated us! Why won't you believe me? Why do you think I lie, when I have to live with this terrible truth, every day of my life?"

"But I –" Stella began.

Her mother didn't stop shouting.

"Get out! You've come all this way just to traumatize both of us. Get out!"

Her screams resounded in the small house, reverberating off the walls, making Stella feel small and helpless and ten years old all over again.

She would get no answers, she realized in despair, as she scrambled to her feet and hurried toward the front door. There were only different versions of lies, which shifted just like the relentless wind battering the dusty panes.

Her mother knew the truth; she was convinced. But she wasn't going to tell, and Stella feared she would take her secrets to her grave.

There was no option now but to leave. She'd have to fly back to New Haven and start her brand new job, and brand new life, without the information and the closure she'd been longing for.

CHAPTER TWO

Two days later.

Stella walked through the front entrance of the FBI headquarters in New Haven. Taking the step through the doorway felt like a life-changing moment. And it was. Over the past few months, her life had changed course in a way she'd never believed would be possible. From today, she was an actual employee here. Ten days ago, she'd graduated from the FBI Academy after winning the Directors Award. Now, she was a field agent in her first-ever posting. It still felt surreal.

As she headed to the security desk to show her new, shiny badge to the guards and complete her sign in process, Stella acknowledged that she wasn't feeling as together as she'd hoped to on her first working day.

The confrontation with her mother had given her confidence a major blow. Rhonda Fall had seemed to be taunting her with the secrets she kept. Her adamant refusal to answer any questions had caused Stella to doubt her own instincts and skills. Stella had left feeling that she was not only a useless investigator, but also a bad and uncaring person. Self-doubt and dark self-criticism had gnawed at her the whole way back to the airport.

Before she boarded, she'd sent her mother a message apologizing for the shortness of her visit and for bringing up the subject of her father again. She'd said she would visit again as soon as she could, and that from next month, she'd be able to wire more money home.

Rhonda had read the message but hadn't responded, and the lack of response was tearing Stella apart.

She didn't want anything to distract from her focus on the first day of such a challenging new career, which would test her abilities and mental strength in every way. She'd hoped that after visiting her mother, she would start her job with a feeling of calmness and a sense of closure. In fact, the disastrous opposite had occurred.

She told herself firmly to get over it. By now, she should know the effect her mother had. There was nothing she could do except wall off the torrent of negative thoughts that overwhelmed her whenever her mind veered in that direction.

"Good morning. I'm New Agent Stella Fall," she introduced herself. The guard passed her the iPad for her to complete her digital registration.

"Morning, Agent Fall," he said formally.

Stella completed the data input, and handed the iPad back to the guard. While he was processing the information, she stared around, taking in the size and scale of the building that was her new workplace.

From now on, if she wasn't out in the field, she would enter this pristine four-story building every day. She guessed its modern and sleek brick frontage had been totally rebuilt from the original offices, constructed in the 1940s.

It was an immaculate, bustling place. A sense of pride emanated from every part of it, the modern reception, the gleaming tiles, the attitude and bearing of the guards and agents. It was thrilling but intimidating to know she was a tiny cog in this giant machine of justice. If she worked her hardest and used her skills to their utmost, she could make a difference in fighting for what was right.

Her signing in was done. Stella realized she wasn't sure where to go now. She'd arrived very early. Supervisory Special Agent Roth, who was her new boss, had said he would meet her at eight a.m. and it was only seven-thirty.

Stella knew where in the building his offices were. Recently, she'd arrived here by helicopter, whisked away from her final week of study at the academy because Clem, her mentor and an ex-FBI special agent, had thought she would have relevant experience in solving a case.

In fact, Stella had ended up solving the case. Roth had praised her highly and as a result, she had earned herself a job working as part of his team. He had needed her skills, and in particular, her psychology background.

Stella headed along the corridor to the section where Roth and his team were stationed. Not that they spent much time in the offices, Roth had emphasized to her. His view was that a field agent should be out in the field. But she was new, so she'd probably not be allowed straight out on cases yet, Stella thought, wondering what the next few months would bring.

She walked into the small lobby where an agent was busy rummaging through one of the filing cabinets. He wasn't someone she had seen before. He looked focused and preoccupied. He found the file he needed, gave her a quick nod, and rushed out again.

There was nothing she could do until Roth arrived. Everyone was busy and she would rather wait for him to introduce her than start roaming around and poking her head into offices to say hi to strangers.

She felt every inch the new girl as she perched on one of the chairs. It brought back old memories of being in high school, and with those in her mind, an idea suddenly occurred to her.

Taking out her phone, Stella scrolled through her messages. She wasn't going to give up on the situation with her mother. She was going to keep demanding answers.

Quickly, she typed out a message.

"Mom, I know you know where Dad is. Don't you think it's unfair to keep it from me? Why would you want to do such a thing? Wouldn't you rather I confronted him in person and found out the real truth? Please, please can you tell me? Because I feel very unhappy and uncertain not knowing."

She read the message. It wasn't the exact tone she wanted, it felt too personal, but she didn't know what the right tone would be. Perhaps confessing to her own vulnerability would touch her mother's heart. Quickly, before she could rethink the idea and decide to abandon it, she pressed Send.

Watching carefully, Stella saw the message had gone through. Her mother had read it, she saw, with a quickening of her pulse. What would she think? Would she reply instantly or would it take a while?

Hearing voices from outside, Stella put her phone away. She jumped to her feet as Roth strode into the room.

Roth's air of harassment preceded him as he rushed into the office. His worried frown didn't ease as he gave a quick nod in her direction. His chestnut brown hair was longer than when she'd last seen it and looked even more overdue for a cut. In the past weeks, Roth hadn't even had time to visit the barber.

She guessed that being a Supervisory Special Agent in this large field office came with more stresses than she could imagine.

"Agent Fall. Welcome to your new workplace. You've arrived on a very busy day." Stella suspected all days were the same as Roth continued hurriedly, "Most of my team are out on cases. This is where you'll be working for the time being."

He indicated the small desk in the only corner of the lobby that was not crammed with wall-to-wall filing cabinets.

"Thank you," Stella said, glancing excitedly at her assigned place of work, and wondering what her first job would be. The desk was completely covered in piles of files. She wondered where they could be moved to.

"As a new agent, I'm sure you want to make a difference."

Stella nodded eagerly.

"However, as a new agent, it's going to be routine for you to handle the day to day tasks that nobody else has time for. Starting with those files." There was a note of humor in his voice as he pointed to them.

Stella looked at the desk again, this time with more concern. What needed doing to these mountains of paperwork? She'd be up for the challenge, of course. It just – wasn't a challenge she'd expected. But Roth was right. Someone had to do the work, and if this was what it took to keep the New Haven office running like a well-oiled machine, then she was the person for the job.

At any rate, Stella tried to cheer herself with this brave internal dialogue.

"These are all recently solved cases, but with our offices going digital, all the information needs to be checked, and then scanned so that there's an online version of each file."

"I see," Stella said, feeling intimidated by the mammoth scope of this task.

"Go through these files and look at the list of contents in the front. Then make sure that all the contents are, in fact, in the file and correctly arranged according to the numbered list. You can't believe how this makes life easier when we urgently need to find a piece of evidence or a witness report – or how much it complicates things when items have gone missing. Then, finally, you can use the computer and scanner in the next-door office to scan each page. Once they're scanned, you save them on the system according to year, month, case name and case number. You'll see how it's done when you start working."

"What do I do if there are any pages missing?" Stella asked.

"The name of the agent in charge of the case is on the front of the folder. Follow up with that agent and ask him for the missing info. Then, once the folders are scanned, they can be manually filed according to the case number."

"I'll make a start now," Stella said, not wanting to show how worried she was by these head-high piles. Instead, she tried to fill herself with positivity, thinking about what a good grounding this would give her in the case histories, and how she'd also get to know the agents in charge if there were any missing pages. So she'd be meeting her colleagues, too!

She looked up, but Roth had already rushed out, leaving her to tackle the first one on her own.

Lifting down the first of probably a hundred folders, she realized the desk was so crammed she couldn't actually work there, so she spent some time rearranging the folders to free up a corner of space. Now the remaining piles were even higher, but in a short time, she would start making a dent in them.

As Stella had the thought, a stressed-looking agent rushed in. Without really looking at her, he raced over to the desk and deposited five new files on top of the pile.

Stella watched in dismay as he hurried out again.

And then, something even worse happened.

From down the passage, she heard a distinctive voice. Sharp and high and resounding with confidence, it sent prickles of instant, unwanted recognition down her spine.

"Where's Supervisory Special Agent Roth? Is he in here? I was told to introduce myself."

Stella felt like taking cover behind the mounds of paperwork. She couldn't, of course.

Instead she watched, appalled, as her tall, lean, confident nemesis strode in.

This was the woman who'd done her utmost to sabotage Stella's journey at Quantico and make sure she didn't qualify as an agent. This was the woman who, shortly before graduation day, Stella had punched in the stomach and knocked off her feet; the gesture causing a bitter and lasting enmity to add to the grudges she already carried.

She'd never dreamed that she would ever see Carrie Potts again!

And, from her equally outraged expression, it was clear that New Agent Carrie Potts had never expected to see her again, either.

CHAPTER THREE

For a long moment, Stella stared at Carrie, seeing her appalled thoughts reflected in the other woman's green eyes.

With a toss of her brunette head and a sneering gaze down her narrow, perfectly shaped nose, Carrie was the first to recover.

"What a surprise to find you here, Stella Fall. My team mentioned to me just now that there was a junior role they had gotten filled."

Her tone was insulting, but Stella could see the insecurity lurking in her eyes.

"How nice to see you," Stella replied evenly. "It sure is a coincidence that we'll both be working here."

Inwardly, she couldn't believe her bad luck. She tried to console herself by remembering that New Haven was a huge office. It was so big that there were satellite offices in the wider Connecticut area. With such a massive operation, hopefully they wouldn't bump into each other too often. Or preferably at all.

Carrie stared at her with a weird, knowing expression.

"Did you ask to be posted here?"

"No, I was offered the job," Stella said shortly.

"That's another coincidence, then. Because a friend of mine was telling me that you're familiar with the area. Is that right?"

She placed a lean finger on her chin as she mulled over her statement.

"Yes, you know I am," Stella retorted impatiently. "I was called here to help with a case in our last week of training. That's how I got to meet Agent Roth."

She stared stonily at Carrie. Carrie hadn't been pleased when she heard Stella had been co-opted onto a case before her training was even done. Had Carrie conveniently forgotten this, or was she just ignoring it?

"Yes, yes, I knew about that. This was something else."

Stella felt a pang of worry. Of course there would be something else. Carrie wasn't baiting the trap for no reason. Unfortunately, her rival was both sharp and perceptive.

"This was something that a friend told me. I have a lot of friends in this area, you know. I'm from Bridgeport originally, which was why I requested a posting to this field office."

"Oh, really?" Stella asked. Now she felt even more concerned.

"That's right. Anyway, a while ago, when I mentioned your name, they said there had been a big scandal earlier this year involving you. My friend's uncle, Gordon Marshall, told her that he couldn't believe the trouble you had caused or how you'd tried to destroy his family. After they suffered a terrible loss, I believe."

Stella's heart stopped.

Carrie had found out about the incident in her recent past that she most wanted to forget. The murder of her fiancé, Vaughn Marshall, had landed her in a world of trouble, and caused her to be the prime suspect for this cold-blooded and violent crime.

This murder was the reason she'd never wanted to return to the state of Connecticut, where the ultra-wealthy and corrupt Marshall family lived. It had been the only factor that had made her hesitate before accepting Roth's job offer.

Now Carrie knew, and this couldn't be more damaging information.

"I believe Gordon has promised that he will get retribution for the pain and suffering you caused, and the way that you tried to smear their good name. Being an ex-senator, he's very influential, as you obviously know," Carrie continued, and Stella felt even more on edge.

Of course revenge would be high on Gordon Marshall's list after she'd exposed the family's misdoings. But she'd never thought that she would be so conveniently situated as a target. She assumed she would vanish from their lives forever and that they would forget about her. Now she was back, and the local network was already buzzing with the news. When Gordon found out where she was working, he would renew his efforts to destroy her.

She was a threat and a danger to him and his corrupt family, and worse still, she was the one who had uncovered their secrets.

Stella was following the news. Their legal team was putting up a fight to try and clear the family's name. With the best lawyers in the state at the Marshalls' disposal, that might well happen.

"You're looking anxious," Carrie said, sounding satisfied.

Stella knew she wasn't. She seldom showed her emotions and had shut down the minute she realized where Carrie's conversation was headed.

"I'm sorry." She gave Carrie a bright smile. "I was focused on the checklist in this folder, and ended up tuning you out. That was rude of me. I do apologize."

Carrie glowered, and Stella felt pleased she had correctly determined that being ignored would trigger her.

"Were you talking about the Marshalls?" Stella then asked innocently. "I guess if I'd really smeared their name, they would have opened a defamation case. Since they haven't done that, perhaps you didn't get all the facts. In any case, it's in the past. I'm not one to hold grudges," she said meaningfully.

She could almost hear Carrie's teeth gritting.

"I don't trust your version, Stella Fall," she spat. "Not after having spent four months at Quantico listening to you twist the truth and manipulate people!"

Stella shrugged. "It's a shame you feel this way," she said neutrally.

Choosing a different angle of attack, Carrie stared at the piles of folders.

"I'll leave you to your paperwork," she said. "I'm sitting with my team this morning and going through some case histories that will be relevant when I start going out into the field. Which, since I was the first new agent to be hired in New Haven this year, will happen soon," she said triumphantly. "They intend to fast-track my career to a fully-fledged field agent as soon as possible. But I'm the first to agree that filing clerks also have value, and I'm very grateful you're here to help our branch with the basic work."

She gave a faux-sweet smile and then turned and stalked out.

Stella let out a long, shaky breath. This couldn't have turned out any worse.

The ultra-competitive and capable Carrie probably would go out in the field before Stella, and she'd clearly been selected for the first available vacancy. Stella had been hired by Roth, but she was a last-minute addition to the team.

All of that meant little compared to the more serious issue that Carrie had friends who were connected to the Marshalls.

This gave her far more leverage to do damage. As soon as she realized how powerful Gordon Marshall was, and how far he would go to try and destroy Stella, she had no doubt that Carrie would use that information to her advantage.

With a sigh, Stella turned back to her filing.

"Oh, Agent Roth!" she heard Carrie exclaim from just outside the lobby. "I wanted to say good morning to you and introduce myself. I'm the new agent, Carrie Potts, who will be working under Special Agent Billings."

In contrast to the poison that had dripped from her tone when addressing Stella, Carrie's voice was now as sweet as sugar, while resounding with all the professional qualities that Stella would have wanted to hear if she'd been a harassed boss.

Clearly, Roth was won over.

"It's great to meet you," he said, and Stella noticed his voice was far warmer than when he'd addressed her earlier. "I look forward to working with you, too. We had excellent feedback on you from Quantico."

"I am so pleased to hear that. And I'll try hard to live up to it. I want you to be proud of me, Agent Roth, and I'm going to do my best for my team."

Humph, Stella thought. She'd never guessed that the haughty Carrie could ever show humility, but it was exactly what she was hearing now.

If only Carrie didn't have a grudge against her, she thought despairingly. Seeing a glimpse of the nicer side that Carrie could clearly show at will, made her feel even worse. Why couldn't she put this enmity aside?

Things had been bad enough between them at Quantico. But in this pressurized work environment, and with Carrie's new-found knowledge about her past, she feared the rivalry might have career-damaging consequences.

Somehow, she would have to manage this potential disaster, as well as deal with all the other complexities of her new job.

She hadn't thought her first day here would be anything like this.

CHAPTER FOUR

Larry Hartford strode out of the Tweed New Haven airport, heading for the pick-up zone where the courtesy driver had just pulled up with his shiny black Mercedes.

He was on the phone with a client, and didn't miss a beat of the conversation as the driver scrambled out, nodding respectfully at Larry as he climbed in.

"Absolutely. We'll sign the franchise territory deal later today and I'll get Garth to make those changes to the contract." Larry quickly tipped the man a fifty and then closed the door. A moment later, his phone connected up with the car's Bluetooth and the client's voice filled the sumptuous, leather-lined space.

"If the changes are made, it's all good."

"Excellent. We're glad to have you on board with Choice Coffees."

Rubbing a hand over his dark, well-cut hair, Larry drove away, dialing his home number as he headed out of the airport.

Being a naturally impatient person, he couldn't suppress a sigh of frustration as he listened to the phone ring and ring. Where was Isabella? He needed to confirm dinner plans, and make sure that she would be okay if they went out with clients. He had a sneaky feeling that this news would not be well received by his gorgeous, blonde, ex-model wife. Especially since it was their anniversary tomorrow, which luckily his PA had reminded him about.

But business was business and these two guys were in town; it was a great opportunity to sweeten them up, maybe even sign the deal. Isabella might be okay with it if he chose somewhere really good.

But if she didn't answer her phone, one of Larry's absolute pet hates, there was no way of moving forward.

"Come on, babes, pick up," he grumbled as he accelerated into the fast lane.

She couldn't be angry with him, could she? Briefly, Larry ran through a mental checklist.

No, she couldn't be angry with him. Yes, this was the third trip in as many weeks but they'd been two nights away at most. And tomorrow night, they really would head out somewhere special for their anniversary. He had the perfect place, chosen and booked by his PA.

"If you would just talk to me, babes, I could organize my life," Larry pleaded, letting out an impatient huff as it rang through to voicemail again.

He couldn't stop a tiny internal flicker of worry.

Was Isabella okay with him? He'd spoken to her briefly yesterday evening and she'd sounded fine. But this morning, when he tried to call before boarding the short flight, she hadn't answered. And now, at quarter to ten, she still wasn't picking up.

She'd spent the previous evening at home. That was what she'd told him. But what if she hadn't? What if that minor fight they'd had before he'd left on his business trip had started bothering her more seriously?

What if she'd left him? What if she'd packed her bags and walked out?

His phone rang just as he was imagining this potential catastrophe. Quickly, he answered, feeling reassured it would be her, calling back.

But he found himself speaking to a random stranger.

"Hello, is that Mr. Hartford?"

"Yes, it is," he snapped, not in the mood for random strangers at this point unless they were potential franchisees, and he could already hear this young guy didn't sound like a potential franchisee.

"I'm at your door with a package. Nobody's home. Would you like us to leave it outside the door or would you prefer us to come back?"

The words tightened a cord of worry, deep in Larry's gut.

"I'll be home in ten minutes. Leave it outside."

Pressing his foot on the accelerator, Larry decided to cut that time down to five minutes. Where was Isabella? Something must have gone wrong. She should have been home, answering her phone, receiving packages. She hadn't had plans this morning; she'd told him so yesterday.

He powered the Merc off the highway, and burned rubber racing onto the main road. He turned right a few streets early to avoid the speed camera, zigzagged his way through the quiet neighborhood. It looked green and serene on this gloomy late October morning. Nothing out of place. Nothing wrong.

Except he feared something was wrong. The dread was constricting his throat and making his hands slip on the smooth leather-lined wheel. The fear of not knowing. Of not being able to predict what he would find when he arrived.

His previous wife had walked out on him. They'd patched things up afterward – briefly, for another month or two, before the marriage had failed completely. But he'd never forgotten that visceral shock of abandonment, of arriving home to find her gone.

He swung the car around the final corner, ignoring the angry blare of a horn from a passing resident, a woman in her Volvo, who stuck her red-tipped hand out the window and made an obscene gesture at him. Larry would normally have flown into a rage and given her a bigger one back. Now he barely noticed.

Isabella leaving was something he'd always dreaded although he'd laughed his own worries off. Why would she ever walk out? She wasn't the same person as Val had been. Besides, she had an easy life; he'd made sure of that. Money to spend on all the luxuries, which she loved. A happy marriage, give or take his workload and the occasional fight.

But still, Larry feared it wasn't good enough. The gnawing in his gut felt suddenly stronger. Ever since flunking out of college, he'd been haunted by the feeling that he was inferior, the feeling that had gotten him up at five a.m. morning after morning, and kept him up till after midnight, night after night, working his way tirelessly up the chain, doing it his way, single-mindedly growing his empire.

He stopped outside the house. The front door was closed. There was the package outside. He buzzed open the garage door. There was her car. But that didn't mean anything; Val had taken a cab when she'd left.

He accelerated in, narrowly missing sideswiping the sleek black BMW as he jolted to a stop inches from the far wall.

He scrambled out and marched into the house. The kitchen was tidy; it didn't look like she'd made breakfast. Hearing the sound of his own breath harsh in the silent room, he hurried into the spacious lounge that Isabella had spent what felt like months decorating to be super-cutting-edge trendy. She'd wanted classic. He'd wanted edgy. He'd won. Now, he wished he hadn't.

"Isabella?" he called. "Izzy?"

No answer.

"Izzy?" he then roared, hearing his voice slam off the walls and reverberate back to him, hearing the panic in his own frantic tone.

She couldn't have left him! She couldn't! Was she in the bath, perhaps? Her phone on silent, maybe she hadn't heard his call? He sprinted upstairs, but the bedroom door was closed, and the bathroom, with its enormous shower and massive spa bath, was empty.

Think, Larry told himself, forcing himself to be calm, trying to suppress the worry that was now making him feel physically sick. Don't shout. She's not answering. Call her again. Maybe this time, she'll pick up. Or maybe you'll hear her phone ring, somewhere in the house.

Taking his own phone out of his pocket, he redialed with shaking hands.

Then he listened carefully for the distinctive, bell-like chimes of her ringtone.

Nothing up here. He rushed from room to room, flinging open the doors. That damned tune, which he'd always complained pierced his brain, resounded through the rooms when it rang. It wasn't up here. Her phone was definitely not on this level of the house.

He rushed downstairs again. Redialed. Listened, straining his ears past the harsh gasps of his own breath.

There it was. That irritating noise. Now, fear clenched his stomach as he heard the distant tune.

It was coming from the large room at the end of the downstairs passage that was fitted out as a fully equipped home gym.

Scenarios flooded his mind as he rushed there. Had Isabella slipped and fallen, bashed her head on the bench? Had she somehow knocked herself out while lifting the free weights that he'd ordered her not to use when she worked out alone because weights needed a partner, apart from when he used them?

Had she gone out of the glass side doors that led into the backyard, and left her phone behind, and had something happened to her out there?

"Izzy?" he yelled as he raced to the gym.

The door was open.

He clutched at the doorframe, skidding to a stop as he saw her there.

She was sprawled on the floor face down in her black lycra shorts, her outflung limbs pale and still.

"Izzy!" he roared again, sprinting through the cool, air-conditioned space to where she lay, feeling a sense of utter disbelief that this was happening. It couldn't be happening!

His wife could not be lying immobile on the floor. He knelt and touched her hand, feeling the chill in her flesh, the stiff immobility of her arm.

He drew in a horrified gasp. Was she dead? She looked dead; she felt dead. This was just impossible – perhaps she could be saved. Perhaps calling an ambulance now would save her.

Fumbling on his keypad, his gasps turned into deep sobs as he started dialing 911. It was only then, staring down at her again, that he saw the worst thing of all.

Larry Hartford let out a cry of utter horror as he saw the black cord, tightly knotted and deeply embedded in the flesh of his wife's neck.

CHAPTER FIVE

Stella was busy with her third folder of the day when she heard a new set of footsteps rushing down the corridor.

After making a small check mark on the list with her pencil so that she could keep track of where she was in the complicated list of documents, she glanced up.

She felt pleased, but also apprehensive, when she saw Special Agent Rick Maxwell rush in.

The dark-haired, muscular and fit agent had been on Roth's team when she'd joined them for the murder investigation a couple of weeks ago. He had resented Stella's presence at first, believing that she'd wrangled her way onto the team through her connections. It had taken him a while to realize that Stella wasn't who he thought she was, didn't have any connections other than her mentor, and genuinely possessed skills the team needed.

She'd ended up respecting Maxwell, and enjoying working with him. Both, a lot more than she'd ever thought she would. Weirdly, at the end of her stint, she'd felt a moment – well, to call it a moment was overstating it. A tingling micro-second when she'd sensed that there could possibly be the chance for something more than friendship between them.

But that had been weeks ago and she'd been a passing stranger. How would he feel now that she was a permanent staff member of the New Haven office? Would they be back to square one in terms of their friendship? Or minus one?

When Maxwell saw her, he stopped in his tracks. The frown of intense concentration on his tanned face dissolved into surprise.

"You're here?"

Stella couldn't tell from his tone whether he thought that was a good thing or not.

"Yes. As of three hours ago," she agreed.

Maxwell paused. Then, to her huge relief, he gave an approving nod.

"It's good to have you on board. Even if you've been stuck with filing duty." He nodded sympathetically at the ranks of folders.

Stella felt encouraged that Maxwell truly was pleased to have her working with him.

"I'm happy to do whatever I need to," she lied, determined to show team spirit even if she longed to be assigned a case immediately. She knew she had to earn her place as a fully-fledged investigator. And going through these files was teaching her a lot about the case procedure and the different aspects that had to be included for them to be fully wrapped up. That was valuable knowledge.

Maxwell seemed about to say something else, but then another set of footsteps, even more rushed, resounded from outside.

Roth appeared. Without Carrie, Stella was relieved to see. Presumably with her introductions now over, her rival had been assigned an equally mundane task. Or so Stella hoped.

"We've got a case that's just been called in. Local PD needs our help urgently."

"Murder?" Stella saw Maxwell's expression harden as he turned.

"Yes. Highly suspicious circumstances, and we have to get involved straight away. The victim is the wife of Larry Hartford, who's a prominent local business leader and also the state governor's nephew. They called us immediately from the governor's office. There's massive political pressure on police and FBI to solve this."

They walked slowly out of the lobby. Roth's voice was lowered as he discussed the details with Maxwell and Stella couldn't overhear what they were. Feeling intrigued and frustrated, she turned back to her checklist, reaching the end of the folder. This was the first file she'd had where everything was in place and she was pleased to see that Maxwell had headed up the case. Clearly, he had an eye for detail. That matched up with his IT and technology background, she remembered.

Then Maxwell's voice rose again, from just outside the doorway.

"Fall could help with this," he said.

Stella sat straighter, quivering with excitement.

Maxwell had actually recommended her? This was incredible! Obviously, Roth would say no. But maybe he wouldn't. Maybe he'd allow her to play some small role.

"It's not really following protocol," Roth said doubtfully.

Stella bit her lip, hoping Maxwell could convince him otherwise.

"We're FBI, and the governor's nephew is involved," Maxwell laughed. "Protocol means solving the case fast. Especially if there are political connections in play; that's even more important."

Political connections gave Stella cause for hesitation. Suddenly she felt less eager to contribute. Was there any relationship between the current governor and a certain ex-senator by the name of Gordon Marshall? Perhaps it would be better for her not to be involved.

"I don't think it's necessary," Roth said doubtfully and Stella felt a rush of relief.

But then, in an undertone, Maxwell continued pleading her case.

Which would it be? She now felt totally conflicted. With the political angle, this was not a good case for her to be involved in. Especially since she was so new, it would be far better to stay right here in the lobby, working on the mountain of files.

As if her thoughts had caused a reverse psychology effect, Roth said briskly, "All right. It may benefit us for her to participate, in a job shadowing capacity."

He strode into the lobby and over to her desk.

"Fall, Maxwell has recommended you get involved in this, strictly as a supervised trainee," he said firmly. "I've agreed, because there are parallels to the previous case where you were able to provide a critical insight."

This was it. She'd been pushed in the deep end. There was no further debate on the matter. And even though her mouth felt dry from nervousness, Stella felt a flame of ambition surge inside her. This was a stepping stone in her career. It was the first case that would be officially linked with her name. It would be an early chance for her to prove herself, and a challenge that she could possibly help solve with the skills she possessed.

"Thank you so much for the chance to come on board. I will do my utmost to help," she said, jumping eagerly to her feet.

Roth regarded the pile of folders thoughtfully for a moment and she wondered if he'd changed his mind. But his next words showed that he was making a different change.

He turned to Maxwell.

"Do me a favor. There's a new agent on the floor above – what's her name?" He frowned briefly before memory served. "Agent Potts. Ask her to come down and carry on with this job. We need to head to the crime scene."

Never had Stella felt so conflicted. It was as if karma had specifically set out to punish Carrie for her earlier taunting. But she couldn't allow herself to feel a moment's pleasure about this. Not when Carrie would now be even more hell-bent on revenge.

Roth detoured to his office to get his briefcase, which allowed Stella to grab her purse and put on her jacket, which she'd slung over the back of the chair.

Then they headed out.

At the foot of the stairs, they passed Carrie. The look she gave Stella was pure, undiluted poison.

*

They piled into Roth's car and headed out. Sitting in the back, Stella felt a weird sense of déjà-vu. This was exactly how it had felt when she'd driven with the two agents to the previous case she'd been involved in. Clem had pressured the academy director, and the New Haven senior directors, to include her. With permission reluctantly granted, she'd felt completely unwanted, a stranger whose presence both Roth and Maxwell resented. Now, she was an official member of the team. Although still a trainee, she felt on a more equal footing with the two men she'd grown to respect.

Even so, the pressure weighed heavily on her. It was so important that she prove herself in this case. What if she wasn't able to add any value, even if the case was similar? It might be speedily solved without any need of what she could contribute.

"So, this is the information we have so far," Roth said, as soon as they'd swung onto the highway. They were heading to the coast, but she had no idea where.

"Larry Hartford is one of Connecticut's biggest movers and shakers. He lives in Branford," Roth explained.

So Stella now knew the area, at least. It was fairly close to the New Haven field office, and far enough from Greenwich, her ex's family's home terrain, to allow her to relax. That was a small relief.

"He's a franchise mogul who owns the rights for several super-successful national franchises. Coffee, pizza, craft beers, convenience stores, to name a few. He's involved in community projects; he's politically connected as you already know. He was away on an overnight business trip in Philadelphia. Flew back this morning and had difficulty contacting his wife from the time he arrived at the airport. He got home and found her in the gym, deceased."

Stella's heart quickened. This was another husband and wife crime. This was why she was included. It was where her experience, rather than her expertise, lay.

From the vicious murder involving her ex-fiancé, to the bloody stabbing case that she'd been co-opted onto thanks to Clem, she'd been unwittingly drawn into a world of conflict, where spouses had secrets, and where nothing was what it seemed.

"Do they know how she died?" she asked nervously.

Please let it not be a stabbing, she begged silently. She didn't think she could handle another stabbing yet. But death was death, she reasoned with herself. No matter the cause, someone had murdered a woman, and violence was inherent in the act.

"She was strangled with a resistance band," Roth said.

"A what?" Maxwell asked, sounding surprised. Stella was glad he'd asked, because she also had no idea.

"It's a form of elasticized rope that can be used as an alternative to weights training," Roth said.

"Ah, okay," Maxwell said.

Stella guessed he was a free weights person. She'd seen people doing yoga and Pilates exercises with elasticized ropes but hadn't known that was what they were called. But, terminology aside, the cause of death raised many concerns. For a start, it was up close and personal. Also, using the equipment on site was spur-of-the-moment, which indicated an unplanned crime.

Roth pulled into a side road. The scenic street, lined with gracious maple trees, was clearly an exclusive residential area. With their exquisite classic and colonial frontages, the stately homes seemed to be frozen in time, but in an understated, rather than ostentatious way, Stella thought. Roth turned the car onto a road which led straight to the beachfront. She stared in awe as he drove. This street ran along a peninsula that overlooked a quiet cove, with sweeping views of Long Island Sound.

Real estate at its most exclusive, she thought, taking in the spectacular sea view.

There were two cars ahead of them on the otherwise empty street, and both turned into the same driveway, heading to a magnificent double-story colonial home.

With its pillared porch and white-painted window frames, the home looked imposing, and yet it fit perfectly into its spacious garden setting, where well-tended shrubs and climbing roses were interspersed with taller trees. The property looked exquisitely maintained. A showpiece house, Stella thought. She wondered if the victim had been a showpiece wife.

"Her name is Isabella Hartford. Husband, Larry, is not a direct suspect, obviously," Roth said.

Stella appreciated his wording. Not being a direct suspect didn't mean that Mr. Hartford hadn't known about it, or been involved. Stella wondered if there had been any trouble between them. Being ultra-wealthy was a complicating factor, as she had personally found out during her brief engagement to Vaughn. Inheritance could have terms and conditions attached, and the threat of disinheritance could be wielded. And a family fortune was often closely linked to a person's ego and perception of themselves. She wondered if the Hartfords' marriage had been happy.

Stella dreaded the emotions that she knew would flare up inside her when they arrived at the scene. Being around shocked, bereaved family would trigger her own grief and trauma from the murder she'd been caught up in, still raw and painful after a few short months.

When she climbed out of the car, she stood for a few minutes, breathing deeply, getting her thoughts and feelings under control.

Then she followed Roth and Maxwell up to the elegant home.

As she approached, she heard a subdued buzz of voices from inside. Entering the home, she saw two detectives wearing protective crime-scene gear walking up the corridor to the left. They looked grim and serious and Stella thought they also looked worried.

Clearly, the pressure to solve this was already bearing down.

Roth stepped forward, greeting his colleagues.

"Morning, Ben. Morning, Eric. I've brought two of my team, agents Maxwell and Fall from New Haven. Where's the foot covers? Can you fill us in on the details?"

Despite the circumstances, Stella felt a moment of pride that, for the first time ever, she was being introduced as a fully-fledged agent and a member of the team. It made her even more motivated to prove herself on this case.

The taller of the two detectives, with graying hair and glasses, headed out of the hall and returned a moment later with a box of gear.

While Stella and the others pulled on the gloves, foot covers and head covers, Ben filled them in.

"They're just wrapping up with the photographing, dusting for prints, and coroner has done a preliminary examination of the body. You're welcome to have a look before they remove it for the postmortem."

"That'll be helpful," Roth said.

"Mr. Hartford is waiting in the outside entertainment area. One of the detectives is there with him. We've done a preliminary interview, about half an hour ago. He was extremely upset and emotional. I'm hoping he's ready to speak to you now."

Stella was listening to the detective's words without really taking them in, because so much of her energy was focused on preparing herself to confront what lay ahead.

The memories of her trauma would never go away and she'd reconciled herself to that. The shock, the terror, the impossibility of finding someone dead. It was making her hands shake and go cold with sweat under the constricting gloves.

"Shall we go through?" Roth asked.

Stella guessed he'd seen so many scenes that he was able to wall it off. Maxwell looked determined, and she figured he was coping with it through his ambitious, competitive nature. His focus was on finding a solution and figuring out who had killed Isabella Hartford.

She had to be the same. Drawing on an inner strength that she knew she was going to need a lot more of in her job, Stella followed them down the elegant passage to the room where the body lay.

CHAPTER SIX

Stella's gaze was drawn straight to the victim's sprawled body when she walked into the gym. Pressing her lips tightly closed, she took in the shocking reality of this death. The woman's outflung limbs, the tawny-gold waves of her hair, glossy and styled.

Who could have done this? Who could have deliberately walked into this palatial and serene home, and ended up murdering her? The impossibility of it made Stella's mind reel.

Isabella was dressed for the gym. She hadn't expected that. What had she expected? She had guessed when hearing about the crime that the woman had walked into the gym and surprised an intruder, who might have broken in through those big, glass doors that overlooked the rolling, green back lawn.

But this looked as if she'd been killed while actually working out.

She narrowed her eyes as she saw the elastic, cruelly drawn around Isabella's slender neck.

Visualizing what might have played out, Stella guessed that the killer would have attacked Isabella from behind and gotten a loop of that thick, strong elastic rope around her neck before she realized what was happening. Pulling that stretchy rope tight would have meant an instant stranglehold and Stella was sure Isabella had panicked; that she'd made the mistake of fighting the rope, trying to pull it away from her throat, rather than trying to damage the person holding it. It would have dug deep in her flesh, cutting off blood as well as air. There would have been a very limited window of time to make the choices that might have saved her life, and Isabella had chosen wrong.

Looking at the woman's right hand, Stella guessed her theory was correct, because two of her long, pearly nails were broken off at the base.

Beside her, Maxwell sighed. "She fought the rope," he said regretfully, and Stella nodded sadly, knowing he'd been thinking exactly the same as her.

Staring at this woman and imagining the crime made Stella feel shaken to her core. But was she missing something? Were there any clues in the surrounding environment?

Looking around, she saw the gym was fully equipped and neat. There were stacks of free weights, and a few more resistance bands hanging from a bracket on the wall. There were two rolled yoga mats, and one unrolled on the floor which again pointed to Isabella preparing for a workout. There was a cross-country ski machine and a treadmill and a rowing machine. Everything looked well used, apart from the spin bike in the corner. That was unplugged, she noticed, and there was a fine layer of dust on the saddle.

Again, her eyes were drawn back to the ropes. The killer had used what was there. Had he or she intended to kill at all? This looked like an impulsive act, triggered by a moment of fury. If you planned on killing someone, you would bring your own weapon with you.

Unless you were a person who was very familiar with the home, and already knew that there would be the perfect weapon waiting, Stella revised her thinking.

"No sign of forced entry," Detective Ben said.

"What about the alarm?" Roth asked.

"There was an internal alarm but it had been turned off," Ben said.

"Time of death?" Roth then queried.

"Between seven-thirty and nine a.m., coroner estimates. Her husband called her from the airport just before nine and she didn't answer. Her phone was in her purse, which was on the shelf near the door. No sign of anything stolen or missing."

The detective was confirming what looked to be the logical conclusion, given Isabella's clothing, and this immaculate gym with nothing out of place and no sign of a struggle. Isabella Hartford had likely been killed by somebody she knew, or at any rate, trusted.

"Let's go and speak to Mr. Hartford now," Roth said.

Stella guessed that he, too, had decided this scene would offer no further clues.

Roth pushed open the glass door, which slid smoothly back, and they stepped out into the autumnal drizzle which was flavored with the tang of the sea.

The entertainment area was across the lawn. Walking in, Stella noticed the comfortable looking wooden furniture, and the gleaming bar across the entire far wall. French doors overlooked a sparkling pool with a rockery and feature waterfall.

Then, feeling her heart clench, she turned her focus to the bereaved husband.

Larry Hartford was a big, solid, dark-haired man wearing a charcoal power suit. He was perched on one of the cushioned sofas, in anguished debate with the detective who was seated opposite.

"I literally have never heard of such a thing happening here. I mean, why me? Why Izzy? How could this happen? I feel like I'm stuck in some kind of nightmare. What are you guys going to do?"

"We're putting all our available resources toward finding your wife's killer," the detective said firmly. Then, looking up and sounding relieved, he added, "The FBI has just arrived."

Larry scrambled to his feet and faced them, breathing hard.

"Please, help me. Help me find out who did this. This is, like, the biggest catastrophe I could ever imagine. I feel like we're wasting time just sitting here! Where's Izzy's murderer now? He could already be miles away! Could have flown out of the country!"

He bunched his hands in agonized frustration.

Stella took in his energy. It was the first thing she noticed. The forcefulness of his character radiated from him, visible in the tension of his face, the restlessness of his body, his rapid breaths.

Upset as he was, she could see Larry was an extrovert, a man of action, and a very dominant person. She guessed that his business success and high profile were largely due to his own tireless efforts.

"We're going to do everything in our power to find out who committed this crime, and arrest the perpetrator as soon as possible," Roth said in a soft voice. "Whatever you can tell us now may be very valuable. Can you take a seat?"

Clearly, Larry didn't want to sit. He lowered himself reluctantly back down on the chair. Roth sat opposite. Maxwell took a seat nearby and Stella joined him on the other end of the couch.

Stella liked the way that Roth was bringing a very calm demeanor to this tense moment. He was balancing out Larry's emotional bluster with a controlled, quiet response that she hoped would have a subtle effect in calming the other man.

"Mr. Hartford, the first thing we need to know is who had access to your home. It's obvious there was no break-in. That means that whoever did this was either working here, or invited here, or else someone your wife felt comfortable letting in."

Looking frazzled, Larry nodded. "I guess so. I guess you're right."

"Do you have household staff?"

"Yeah, we have a housekeeper. She should be here by now. I don't know where she is."

Was her unscheduled absence significant, Stella wondered?

"Then we have a pool maintenance guy who comes twice a week, Mondays and Thursdays. And there's a gardener who works Monday to Friday."

"Where is he now?" Roth asked.

There was no sign of a gardener in the grounds, Stella noted, feeling suspicious.

"I – uh, I don't know. I don't know where he is today. I can give you his number."

"How long has he worked for you?"

"For two years. Since we moved here, basically. The housekeeper also. The pool man's been with us about a year. We rebuilt the pool a year ago."

Larry rubbed a hand over his face. Stella thought about what he'd said. The absence of the cleaner and gardener was strange. The whereabouts of these staff was a clue that needed to be followed up.

"Any problems with any service provider? Do you recall your wife mentioning anything unusual? Any money issues, any complaints?"

Roth was already pursuing this angle, seeking potential motives.

"No, seriously, I don't remember a thing being wrong. Besides, Izzy didn't really manage the staff. That's the housekeeper's job."

Interesting, Stella thought. Clearly, that statement prompted another line of questioning from Maxwell, who cleared his throat.

"What did your wife do during the day, Mr. Hartford?" Even though Stella knew that Maxwell had a healthy disrespect for people who didn't put in the hard hours to earn their keep, he kept his voice low and polite as he asked, "Did she work, full-time or part-time?"

"No, no, she didn't need to. Wouldn't have had time," Larry explained, blinking hard as if another wave of reality was overwhelming him. "She was very busy. She is – was – an ex-model. She did a lot of mentoring of young people, free training for girls who wanted to model. She taught modeling a few hours a week at a local arts and acting school. She worked with charities that helped the underprivileged to get access to education, opportunities, training. She kept herself in shape, did a lot of working out. Spin classes, that sort of thing. She liked her spin classes."

Stella remembered the cycling machine out in the home gym, that dust-covered spin bike. Perhaps Isabella had enjoyed group classes rather than working out on her own.

"Did you two socialize a lot?" Roth then asked. Stella could see this question opened the door to asking about their relationship.

"Yeah, yeah, just about nonstop. When I was in town, with my business commitments and all, we had client dinners and events at least four times a week. Charity functions, also. And my uncle often invites us to openings, launches, that sort of thing."

"What about your friends?" Stella asked.

These was the first words she'd spoken, and Larry turned to glance at her in a semi-distracted way.

"Yeah, we had friends, of course. I must say, though, we were both so busy we didn't really have time to see them that much."

A brief silence fell, and Stella found herself thinking about those words with a degree of sadness and sympathy.

She thought Larry's account spoke of a fast-paced, but yet superficial and somehow unfulfilled life. A 'social whirl' did not mean that meaningful connections were being made. In particular, none of Isabella's friends had yet been mentioned, and Stella guessed that her needs were overshadowed by his.

Perhaps her daytime activities had included the things she enjoyed, seeing as how the evenings seemed to be dominated by Larry's business events.

"What was your marriage like?" Roth asked. Stella listened carefully to Larry's response to this important question.

"Well, it was okay. Good, I think. She was my second wife. I'm thirty-five, so ten years older. My ex remarried and moved to Florida. We've been married almost two years and everything seemed good. I mean, she seemed happy. She didn't complain. She didn't have family here – her mother and sister live in San Francisco, and I know that was the one thing she would have liked: more time to see them. Apart from that, everything was fine, I think. I thought."

He gulped.

Stella looked down, not wanting to watch as a surge of grief hit him. She saw Roth and Maxwell doing the same thing, briefly glancing away, and felt glad that her team was showing a level of compassion she respected.

"Did you have any fights recently?" Maxwell then asked, once Larry had taken a few deep, gasping breaths.

"No, no. I mean, arguments, yes. We always used to disagree; it was like a standing joke between us. I'd say one thing, she'd say another. But no bad fights. Our anniversary was tomorrow. I'd already booked a good place; we were going to have a great night. We both enjoyed eating out, the whole social scene."

Stella wondered briefly if the upcoming anniversary had been significant in any way, or just a coincidence. Was Larry mentioning it to try and prove to them, or even to himself, that nothing serious had been wrong?

"So divorce was not in the cards?" Roth asked, echoing her suspicions.

Larry looked surprised. "Divorce? No, no, I mean we fought, but not badly. And I've been divorced, so I know how bad things can get. We were happy together."

"Did you get on well with the neighbors?" Stella asked.

Larry shrugged. "Isabella might have known them better than me. We didn't socialize with them, if that's what you're asking. But we are friendly with them, if we see each other, we'll wave and suchlike."

Roth gave a firm nod at this question, and Stella guessed that the neighbors would be next on the list to question.

"Does your home have security cameras?" he then asked, and Stella also sensed that this was a final question and that he was wrapping up what he wanted to say.

Larry shook his head. "We never thought we needed cameras. Our alarm system worked well. When it was turned on."

He briefly sunk his head into his hands and Stella could see that yet again, he felt overwhelmed by what had happened.

"Do you have someone who can be with you now?" Stella asked.

Larry nodded, looking distracted. "My sister lives in Fall River. She's on her way here, as we speak."

"Thank you for your help," Roth said, standing up as he concluded the interview. "I appreciate it's an extremely difficult time for you. We may need to speak to you again to confirm further details, and if so, we'll call you, so please keep your phone with you or make sure the police have your sister's number."

"I will." Larry also rose to his feet, his restless energy surging again. "Appreciate you guys being on the case. Anything to make sure this killer is found. Anything." His voice sounded agonized. As she walked away, Stella felt it tug a cord of sympathy deep within her.

She knew exactly how Larry felt. How shocked, how helpless.

But, as an investigator, she also had to remember this could be a convincing act. Larry had an alibi and hadn't committed his wife's murder himself, although she was sure Roth would check he really had been on that flight.

Despite Larry's protests that their marriage had been happy, that didn't mean it really had been. People had hidden depths. Stella couldn't rule out that this wealthy and controlling man might have organized the crime.

She couldn't wait to hear if Roth shared her suspicions.

CHAPTER SEVEN

Quietly, they walked out, bypassing the gym where Stella saw with a lurch of her stomach that Isabella's body was now being removed. She didn't want to see it again and was thankful when they headed directly across the lawn instead.

"Do you think Larry could have organized it, as a hit? Could Isabel have had an affair, or wanted a divorce?" she murmured to Roth as they headed out.

"We can't rule out that possibility," Roth agreed. "I was also doubtful about how happy that marriage really was."

Stella felt glad that her own suspicions were vindicated.

But Roth continued in a warning tone, "However, that doesn't mean that her husband wanted to kill her. Remember, we can't pursue one theory to the exclusion of other evidence. At this stage, there's a lot of evidence still to be gathered before we can start to see which directions are the strongest. We do need to keep their relationship top of mind, and get others' views on it. That will lead us to a conclusion and there'll be more to guide us."

Stella nodded, curbing her impatience. Roth was right. There was a lot of evidence still missing for the bigger picture to be seen.

There were now a few cars parked outside the home in addition to the mortuary van. The scene was attracting attention. It wouldn't be difficult to speak to the neighbors, seeing the front doors of the homes on either side were open, and a woman was at the garden gate of the house opposite.

"Now will be a good time to engage with the neighbors," Roth decided. "I'm going to talk to the people on the left. Maxwell, you take the right. Fall, you head across the road. Once we're done, we can meet back here and compare notes. We'll then decide on the next step."

Glad that the rain had cleared, Stella quickly crossed the road, and greeted the opposite neighbor, who was a woman with shiny, steel-gray hair. She wore a plush crimson jacket, and stylish tan boots.

"Good afternoon," Stella said, realizing to her own surprise it must be afternoon by now.

"Afternoon," the woman said, a questioning note in her voice. She stared at Stella curiously.

"I'm FBI Agent Stella Fall," Stella introduced herself.

"You are?" the woman said, sounding surprised. "Well. Nice to see a woman agent. I'm Marion Pinner. I guess if you're here, that means that there has been a serious crime at the Hartfords?" she added, sounding anxious.

"Unfortunately, Mrs. Hartford has been murdered," Stella said in a low voice.

Marion clapped a slim-fingered hand over her mouth. "Good heavens!"

Her thick gold rings gleamed in the dull afternoon light as she slowly lowered her hand again and placed it on the gate. "I'm shocked. How can such a thing happen here?" she added incredulously.

"It's shocking and tragic," Stella agreed in a sympathetic tone. "This is a top priority case, and we hope to have answers soon. Did you know the Hartfords at all?"

"Not well. I used to see Mrs. Hartford quite often, as I'm a gardener." She gestured briefly at the rolling lawn behind her. Stella nodded, surprised that Marion clearly did a lot of work on the immaculate flower beds herself. "She was always coming and going. A very pretty woman, and friendly. She'd often wave at me as she left, and I'd wave back. It made the day brighter to greet each other. I thought of her as a friend I'd never properly met," she said sadly.

Before Stella could steer the conversation around to their interactions, Marion drew herself up as if she felt she had to ask the question, and blurted out, "How did she die? Do they know – who killed her?"

In her eyes, Stella could see a desperate need for answers, but also fear – the fear that there was a random killer in the neighborhood.

Not wanting to give too many details, she simply said, "The coroner will need to confirm the cause of death, and Isabella's next of kin be notified, before we can make any facts public. However, I can confirm that there was no sign of forced entry."

Marion nodded, her eyes wide and serious. "So she was killed by someone who knew her? Isn't that shocking? Just so impossible!"

"We're looking for any background information that could lead us to the killer," Stella said. "Did you ever speak to Isabella? Or notice anything unusual happening – any fights you might have overhead, anything out of the ordinary?"

There was silence for a while, broken only by the crackle of walkie-talkies from across the road, and the thrumming of the wind in the branches of the stately oak tree near Marion's garden gate.

Marion was frowning thoughtfully.

"You know, I did speak to her a while ago, when I met her in town. It wasn't a long conversation."

"How recently was that?" Stella asked.

"Not so long ago. A couple of months, maybe. She was going into the hairdresser and I was heading out. We recognized each other, and stopped at the door and chatted for a minute."

"What did you speak about?" Stella asked.

"Well, she was kind enough to compliment my hair. I thanked her and asked how she was enjoying the weather – it was a perfect summer morning. She replied very politely that she would be enjoying it more if she could have gone on a vacation that her husband hadn't canceled due to work. She sounded quite bitter about it."

"Really?" Stella questioned, feeling her spine tingle.

"I got the impression she was discontented with her life. You know, when someone's happy you can usually tell instantly. And when someone's got issues, you can tell, too. I know she used to be a top model. One of my daughter's businesses is a fashion boutique so we keep up to date on that. She worked for a couple of the luxury brands. I believe she struggled with her weight, though, according to the tabloids. Weight was always an issue and the reason she decided to quit the industry," Marion sighed. "Perhaps she found being a stay-at-home wife was stifling. And of course, Larry would have been the decision maker, with all his business activities. Now I wish I'd asked her more."

"Did you see her this morning? Or notice anyone coming or going?" Stella asked.

She hoped that Marion might have seen something, given her love for gardening and the fact that she noticed activity next door.

"I headed out just before eight this morning," Marion said. "When I left, I did notice a red car driving onto our road, going very slowly. I remember wondering if they were lost, or looking for a house."

"Do you know what kind of car?" Stella asked.

Marion shook her head. "I think it was an SUV, a bigger type of car. That's what made me think it was a visitor, rather than a delivery person."

A red car. Well, at least it was something. Stella hoped this detail could prove useful.

"Do you have any security cameras that overlook the road?" she asked.

"No, unfortunately not. We have security beams surrounding our house, and an alarm system. No cameras."

Stella nodded. "Thank you very much for the information. If you remember anything else about the car, will you give me a call?"

She was too new to have business cards, she realized, so instead she tore a page off her notepad and wrote her phone number on it.

"Here you are. Please, get in touch if you think of anything else. The smallest detail might be helpful."

"I will do," Marion promised.

Stella walked back to where Roth was standing at the front door.

They moved into the house and stood in the hallway, discussing their findings quietly.

"I didn't get anything from the northern neighbors," he said. "What did you find out?"

"The neighbor opposite saw a red SUV, driving slowly in the direction of the Hartfords' house, before eight this morning."

"Okay." Roth didn't sound as if this was game-changing information. Stella guessed it was too vague to be of real use.

"She bumped into Isabella a while ago, at the hairdresser, where she complained they'd had to cancel a vacation because of Larry's work. She had the sense that things weren't going right."

"Interesting, but not conclusive," Roth said.

"I get the impression she was in a very controlling relationship. Even if Larry Hartford didn't realize it. It seemed like he called the shots," Stella said.

"Yes, I definitely got the sense he's a bombastic man who does things his way," Roth agreed.

"I wonder if Isabella had an affair," Stella said. "Do you think a lover could have murdered her? I mean, she was discontented in her marriage, there was no forced entry and no sign of a struggle."

"It's certainly a possibility," Roth agreed.

A possibility? Stella felt disappointed. She was pleased by her reasoning. However, Roth's words reminded her that suspicions, though they might be valid, needed to be backed up by hard evidence.

At that moment, Maxwell headed inside.

"What did you get?" Roth asked.

"They have cameras but not on the road. The husband and wife were both home this morning but they were indoors, unfortunately," Maxwell said.

"Any impressions of the Hartfords?"

Maxwell nodded. "The wife used to greet Isabella across the hedge, usually when she was swimming or tanning. She said that she seemed a bit offish the last few times they spoke. She was wondering if something was wrong, but wasn't on a close enough footing with her to ask."

"That's similar to what Marion said," Stella observed.

"But it's minor. We're talking about being discontented in some way. It might not mean much," Roth warned. "Even so, we must keep it in mind as we look for more evidence. And that's what we're going to do now. I've got a list of the contact numbers of all employees who work at the house, so we can confirm their whereabouts this morning and hopefully get some information from them, too."

"What about Isabella's phone?" Maxwell asked. "We need her call records."

"It's locked," Roth said. "Larry has no idea of the code. So we're sending it to one of our techs who'll unlock it. He's good, so that will be done within a few hours, probably."

At that moment, there was a minor commotion from outside. Stella heard raised voices, and then a woman's voice, high and shocked, crying out.

"What are you saying? Dead? It can't be! How could this have happened?"

They all exchanged a surprised glance before rushing to the door.

CHAPTER EIGHT

Outside the Hartfords' front door, Stella saw a sturdy, dark-haired woman had arrived. She was doubled over in hysterical tears. One of the detectives was holding her arm and she guessed that without this supportive grasp, the woman would have actually collapsed onto the immaculate slate paving stones.

"This is Asoese Lee, the Hartfords' housekeeper," the detective muttered to Roth.

Asoese looked to be in severe shock. Stella took her other arm and they guided the loudly sobbing woman inside, away from the curious stares of the onlookers.

"Let's sit you down in the lounge," the detective decided, and they went through the double doorway into the ultra-modern lounge.

While the detective was getting Asoese seated, Roth drew Stella aside.

"I'd like you to question her as soon as she's calmed down. I think she'll respond better to a one-on-one. Maxwell and I will wait in the dining room. We're going to go through the list the detectives have given us, make a few calls, confirm what we can immediately."

"I'll do that," Stella said.

At the far end of the lounge was a fully stocked bar. Stella saw some bottles of mineral water there. She hurried to the bar, poured a glass of water, grabbed some paper towels, returned to Asoese, and sat down beside her.

"I'm so sorry about this," she said quietly, offering the water.

Asoese grasped the glass in both of her shaking hands.

Drinking a few sips helped her calm down. When her breathing was less ragged, Stella took the glass back and handed her a paper towel.

Asoese blew her nose hard, wiped her eyes, crumpled the towel, and stared at Stella, blinking rapidly.

"I'm Special Agent Stella Fall from the FBI," she introduced herself.

"I – I'm Asoese. I work here. I arrived for work and they told me Mrs. Hartford was killed this morning."

Stella saw appeal, as well as fresh tears, in her reddened eyes. Perhaps she was hoping Stella might correct her and say it was a mistake, and the worst had not happened. All she could do in response was nod gravely to confirm the tragedy.

"This cannot be real," Asoese muttered. "When did it happen?"

"Earlier this morning." Stella decided this would be a good lead-in to discuss Asoese's whereabouts. "What time do you usually arrive at work?"

"This morning? So recent? I am normally here by eight." Asoese considered this information with an appalled expression, realizing what might have been.

Stella waited patiently for Asoese to get over her renewed shock at the timing. After a pause, she spoke again in an unsteady voice.

"I got permission from Mrs. Hartford to arrive later this week. My daughter has just moved to a closer school, and I wanted to walk there with her for the first few days, to make sure she was settled in." Then, sounding more concerned, she added,"Do you need proof of this?"

"Yes. Please provide proof if you have it," Stella said. "It will be very helpful."

Asoese fumbled in her purse.

"I can show you photos? These I took this morning, just before catching the bus to come here. Here are my daughter and I, outside the school gates."

Quickly, she scrolled through her gallery and showed Stella the most recent shots. In them, Asoese was standing next to a slim, dark-haired girl who looked about twelve years old. Asoese was wearing the same mauve top, and the same pink lipstick as she was now. She was smiling happily, clearly unaware of the traumatic events about to unfold.

"How far away from here do you live?" Stella asked, for final confirmation of what looked like a solid alibi.

"It's a forty-five minute trip from my house to here. I usually use the bus and train. By car, it's slightly faster," Asoese explained.

Now she was sounding more settled, and Stella guessed the initial hammer blow of shock had passed.

Thanks to the photographic proof, Asoese was not a suspect, Stella decided, but she might have valuable information about Isabella's recent activities.

"We are looking into Mrs. Hartford's private life," Stella explained gently, with her suspicions about the affair uppermost in her mind again. "Do you know if there were any recent problems in her life, or anything unusual happening?"

"She was always so busy," Asoese said with a sigh. "I did not know everything she did. There was the model training, at the art school in New Haven. She loved that, even though some of the events were after hours and she was angry when she had to cancel because of other plans. And her spin classes. She used to attend those in the afternoons, mostly."

Stella decided this was more proof of Larry's control.

"You say she attended spin classes regularly?" she asked, recalling that Larry had also mentioned them.

"She started them a few months ago, and used to go about five days a week. They were very important to her. She said they were the best fitness and weight loss class she knew of."

"Do you know what the class was called?" Stella felt hopeful that if Isabella was such a good regular there, she would have made friends who might know more about her personal life.

She could see Asoese was thinking hard, frowning as if the events of the morning had derailed her memory.

"I remember. Spirit Spin," Asoese said, sounding relieved.

After making a note of the name, Stella decided it was time to tread over more sensitive ground.

"Do you think Mrs. Hartford was happy in her marriage?"

Asoese paused for a few moments. She frowned, biting her lip doubtfully.

Stella felt a flash of excitement, because a simple 'yes' would have been easy to say and taken no time at all. The fact that Asoese was hesitating, choosing her words, was already a red flag.

"She was not unhappy," she said carefully.

"Anything you say will remain confidential," Stella said. "We will not tell anyone. This conversation is private."

She felt sure that Asoese was thinking of her future job prospects and did not want to speak badly of her employer – who, ultimately, was Larry.

Asoese grimaced. "I do not think she was happy. They fought a lot. He would often walk out after a fight, and there were times when I overheard her shouting at him on the phone," she said, in a soft apologetic voice.

"Did she ever mention divorce? To you, to anyone, to a friend?" Stella asked.

Asoese was silent for a moment.

"I don't recall her mentioning divorce, but she did not speak about personal issues with me. In fact, for the past few weeks, I noticed things seemed better between them and they were fighting less than they had done."

That was interesting, too, Stella noted. Perhaps it pointed to an affair – or else, that Isabella had made her own private decisions about what to do.

"That's everything I need to ask. The police may want to check other information with you. I'll call them now. Thank you for being so helpful, in such a difficult time," Stella said gently.

She stood up and quietly left the room.

The detective was waiting outside.

"I've said you may also want to speak to her. She's calmed down now, and has a confirmed alibi and a reason for arriving late," Stella told him, before hurrying through to the dining room.

There, Roth and Maxwell had set up their laptops on the table. Maxwell was concluding a phone call and Roth was making notes on a pad.

"The flights are confirmed. Mr. Hartford was in Philadelphia at the stated time," Roth said.

"The pool boy has an alibi," Maxwell said, disconnecting. "He was cleaning a pool in Greenwich, which from his description, sounds about the size of a small ocean. He was busy from seven a.m. for the whole morning with that customer, and to confirm this, he's forwarding me screen shots of their online conversation. Oh, here they are." Maxwell glanced down and sighed cynically. "Flirty," he concluded in resigned tones. "I'll try the gardener next."

Roth turned to Stella.

"How did your interview go?"

"Asoese Lee has a confirmed alibi and had asked for permission to arrive late today. She also thought Isabella's marriage was unhappy. She mentioned the spin class was very important to Isabella. It could be a good place to find people who knew her. I'd like to look it up. Can I use one of these?"

"Sure." Maxwell turned the closer laptop toward her. Stella took the chair next to him, and looked up Spirit Spin.

"Wellness. Balance. Weight loss. Strength. Togetherness. Join the Spirit Spin vibe in West Haven, CT, and become part of our fitness family!" the website promised, confirming every possible selling point

of the class. The website also gave the times of the classes. There were two morning classes, at six-thirty a.m. and nine-thirty a.m., and an afternoon class at three p.m. Classes were Monday to Friday only. *"Private lessons upon request on evenings and weekends,"* the website said.

It seemed as if these classes were definitely geared toward clients who didn't have a day job, Stella thought, as two of the three scheduled classes were at times when the average person would be at work.

She was astonished to see the prices of the group classes. These were seriously expensive! Most definitely, Spirit Spin's target market was people who had money to burn.

Checking the time, Stella noted that the afternoon class would already be under way.

She wrote the address down, and as she looked up, she saw Maxwell make a face.

"I can't get hold of the gardener. His phone's off."

Stella remembered that the gardener was supposed to work Monday to Friday. His absence, together with the switched off phone, was a red flag.

"We need to pull his home address," Maxwell said.

"I'll get onto that," Roth agreed. "Any luck with the spin classes, Fall?"

"The spin school is in West Haven, and there's a class under way now. I think we should take a drive there."

Roth nodded. "You two go ahead. I'll let you know as soon as there's more information on the gardener."

Stella felt relieved to be heading out of the Hartfords' home, where the bustling in and out of the hallway and crackle of walkie-talkies had become a background noise as the police went about their work. And she felt surprisingly amped to be paired up with Maxwell. They'd done a fair amount of investigation together in the previous case and they'd worked together well. She liked the energy between them. Was it more than just a good working relationship? Stella wondered, before suppressing that feeling. They were on a murder case and she needed to focus on the matters at hand. This was not the time to even think of the spark she occasionally sensed when they looked at each other.

Instead, she thought about what to say, and how to approach the topic, when they arrived at Spirit Spin. She hoped Isabella's spin friends would be able to give more insight into the possible causes of her murder.

CHAPTER NINE

Music thumped in Stella's eardrums as she approached the large brick building, which, from the vivid branding on the walls, seemed to be dedicated solely to the spin classes. The parking lot was crammed with luxury cars. The unmarked Ford that she and Maxwell had arrived in looked small and humble next to the gleaming array of sports vehicles and SUVs.

"Quite the destination," Maxwell remarked, sounding surprised.

"Isn't it?" Stella replied.

The beat grew louder as she and Maxwell neared the open door and headed into the lobby. Above the throbbing trance music, a man's deep, compelling tones resounded over a loudspeaker.

"Arm lifts. Reach for the sky! Thrust those weights up. Don't just lift. Thrust! And – one, two, three, four…"

Stella blinked in surprise as she pushed the heavy studio door open. This was more like a nightclub than a gym class. The enormous, dimly lit studio was brightened by flashing overhead lights, glowing red strobes, and laser beams. The music was so loud it seemed to reverberate through every cell of her body. Above it, the man's voice sounded again, clear and rich, over what must be a seriously good loudspeaker system.

"And pump that left arm. While you pedal. Pedal and pump! Pedal and pump! Thrust that weight high. One, two, three, four. Get those hands up, curl them down. Five, six, seven, eight. Feel the burn. Push through the pain. You need to focus on your goals. Focus on what's waiting for you. Remember, when your limbs are tired, your heart will take you where you want to go. And pedal fast for eight now, while you work your right arm."

Now that Stella's eyes had adjusted from the bright outdoors, she could see that the room was filled with state-of-the-art spin bikes, positioned a couple of yards away from each other. There must be thirty bikes in total, she guessed. In front of each bike was a rack with a small selection of weights on it. The bikes all faced a platform, behind which was a screen where shifting neon patterns were swirling on a dark background.

The women clutched weights in each hand while they pedaled furiously. Stella could almost taste the sweat and raw effort as they rode.

She glanced at Maxwell, who was surveying the scene incredulously. He was so caught up in viewing this spectacle that he didn't even notice her looking at him.

Turning back to the room, Stella then noticed that there was a bike on the platform. So this was where the instructor rode, but where was he?

Glancing around, she found him with some difficulty in the dark, laser-lit space.

The tall, fit-looking instructor was moving swiftly from bike to bike, carefully correcting the riders' posture with expert caresses of his hands.

As she watched, he stepped onto the stage again and jumped onto his own bike, lifting a pair of heavy weights with ease.

"And now, we finish with the twists. Raise both hands and stretch them out to your sides. As far as you can go. I don't want those arms to move. Don't allow your arms to feel weakness. And now, we twist left. Left, left, feel the burn. Don't bounce, push. Hold. And don't slow your pedaling. Keep that rhythm."

With the lights playing off his defined arms, he was a compelling class leader, Stella saw.

"And we twist right. And we will do it eight times each way. Left. Hold it, hold it, don't let those arms relax. I can see some of you want to rest. Rest does not make progress. And right. Twist right. Work all those lateral muscles. Feel your belly firm, your core tighten. This is what will make you not just fit, but iron-hard. And left."

Narrowing her eyes against the spiraling lights, Stella saw the women's arms were beginning to shake. Keeping those weights stretched outward must be excruciating.

Then, as if on cue, the music slowed and softened.

"Weights on the rack. Place them there with respect. They worked for you, they bettered you. Now ease off on the pedal tension. Stretch those muscles out. Stretch sideways, stretch up, ease your necks, circle your shoulders. Slower, slower, let your legs wind down. Thank your beautiful legs for the work they have done. Thank them for being tough and strong, like your hearts. Like your spirits. You have proved this to me. You have showed me your strength and your heart this afternoon.

You put your love into this class. You are beautiful, inside and out. And now, now, we stop."

Stella couldn't quite believe that a group of women were honestly buying into this talk during a fitness class, but the ladies seemed hypnotized by the mellow-voiced encouragement. She saw several of the women collapse over the handlebars as soon as they heard the word 'stop.'

Gradually, the music reduced to background level. Over it, breathless voices and laughter became audible as the participants scrambled off their bikes.

"That was the hardest one yet!"

"I'm done! Anyone want to carry me out?"

"Did you manage all the arm lifts? I only did half of the last set. I just couldn't. Next time!"

With the music down, the lights were then brightened, transforming the large space from its nightclub vibe into a more normal looking fitness room.

Stella noted that about half the bikes were occupied, and the class was made up exclusively of women, who all looked to be the same echelon as Isabella. Slim, gorgeous, and clearly motivated to work on their physical appearance. She saw sweat-dampened, but still glamorous, wavy locks, and exquisite lycra outfits that hugged their shapely bodies. Arduous though the class had been, many of the women still wore their gold jewelry and earrings.

The instructor was working the room again, offering tender shoulder massages and thigh rubs to his weary students. He was seriously good-looking, Stella saw. Now that the lights were brighter she could take in his perfect bone structure, strong jaw, and defined build. The black handlebar vest and skin-tight shorts he wore showed off his ripped limbs to the max.

Moving from client to client, he was the recipient of grateful smiles and breathless thank-yous, Stella saw.

He grinned at the woman he was massaging, gently easing her long ponytail aside as he rubbed her back, his teeth flashing white in his tanned face. Then they got into an animated conversation which seemed to center around one of the exercises. Stella was too far away to hear.

But then, the woman on the bike at the back of the room turned around and noticed her. The attractive brunette gave Stella a curious stare. Her perfectly micro-bladed eyebrows raised slightly when she saw Maxwell. Clearly, male intrusion into this female class was unusual.

"Hi there. Are you looking for Trevor?" she asked.

Maxwell stepped closer and said quietly, "We're FBI Agents Maxwell and Fall. We're investigating Isabella Hartford's death. I understand she was a regular at these classes? We came here to see if we could speak to some people who knew her well."

Instantly, the woman's face changed. She shook her head sadly, looking upset.

"It's such a tragedy. We are all so shocked. Trevor said he couldn't believe it when he got the call."

"How did he hear about it?" Maxwell asked.

"He told us he heard from one of Isabella's colleagues at the arts school. She didn't arrive for a meeting, so they called her home number, and found out."

"It must have been a terrible shock," Stella agreed.

"I actually wondered whether I should even come to class today, but I thought it was important for us to be together and support each other at this time." She undid her ponytail and shook out her glossy hair. "There are a couple of afternoon regulars who I see stayed away today. Please, anything I can do to help you, I will."

Stella made a mental note to find out more about the missing regulars. There could be a more suspicious reason for their absence.

"What's your name?" Maxwell asked.

"I'm Helen van der Meulen. I've been doing Spirit Spin ever since it opened up here. It must be nearly three years now. It's changed my life, I must say. What a fantastic class it is!" she said enthusiastically.

"Did you know Isabella well?" Maxwell continued.

Helen shook her head. "We weren't really in the same group of friends. We would always say hello in passing, but with such a big class, and all of us busy people, we didn't have the time to get to know everyone else personally. Now I wish I had. I feel so traumatized about what has happened," she explained sadly.

"Who were her close friends?" he asked.

"Barbs and Jasmine are the two I saw her with the most. They're the two regulars I noticed aren't here today. But I have Barbs' number, if you want it?"

"Please," Maxwell said.

Helen walked over to the row of lockers and opened one. She took out her phone and read the number to him.

The class was emptying out. People were grabbing their gym bags and leaving. A couple had headed for the showers, but the majority were simply heading out as they were. Going straight home to more luxurious bathrooms, she guessed.

"I'm so glad to see it's already being investigated," Helen said. "I think it will give us all peace of mind once we have closure."

"It's a top priority case, ma'am," Maxwell reassured her.

As Helen left, Maxwell tapped Stella's arm.

"Let's speak to the instructor," he said in a low voice.

Stella wanted to speak to him, too. She hadn't thought his classes would be so immersive. There was a level of personal involvement with his clients that she hadn't expected to see. It intrigued her, especially since Isabella had been such a dedicated fan of these classes.

With his clients leaving, the fit-looking man was straightening things up after the class. He was moving from bike to bike with a bucket and cleaning cloths, carefully spraying them down, wiping the weights, and arranging them tidily on their holders.

Stella and Maxwell headed over to him. The lavender-scented fragrance of the disinfectant filled the air as they approached.

The man looked up inquiringly.

"Good afternoon," he said. "How can I help?"

"Agents Fall and Maxwell from the FBI," Maxwell introduced them.

The man's eyebrows raised.

"You're here already? I'm relieved the police are acting on this tragedy so fast. What a terrible thing it is. I'm Trevor Urban, and I own Spirit Spin. I can tell you right now that this has been a huge blow to our fitness community. It's devastated all of us! Isabella was a valued client, and a much loved member of the class."

Stella had to force herself to look away from his hazel-eyed stare, which was strangely hypnotic. Although his voice was warm, his eyes were surprisingly blank, and his gaze seemed to drill into her, as if Trevor was used to assessing his guests and picking up subliminal information about them. That made her feel disturbed.

She suddenly realized that even though Maxwell had introduced them, Trevor had made immediate eye contact with her. Despite the fact she hadn't spoken a word to him directly yet.

Perhaps she was more his target market than Maxwell was. You didn't get to build a successful and very expensive niche exercise business without automatically turning the charm onto potential customers, she thought wryly.

"I nearly canceled classes today when I heard, but I thought that our loyal regulars would draw some comfort from being with each other in a supportive environment," he explained to Stella.

"How long had Isabella been attending your classes?" Stella asked. She decided since she was his focus of attention, she should take the lead in questioning him, as it was obvious he would speak to her more readily.

"If I recall, we welcomed her into the group about five or six months ago," Trevor said in tones of hushed respect. "She'd been attending spin classes at her local gym, and then someone recommended me. I would have to check my records for an exact date."

"Did she ever chat with you on a social level, outside of class?" Stella asked.

Trevor smiled. The expression was sad, conveying genuine regret, but it still didn't reach those calculating eyes.

"I guess you're hoping that I might have some information on her private life that could lead to her killer. How I wish I did!" He spread his muscular arms sadly. "I take the time to get to know every individual in my group, because their fitness journeys are all very close to my heart. I take such pride in seeing them grow, become stronger – mentally, as well as physically."

Stella waited for Trevor to finish the elaboration. He sure wasn't skimping on the detail, she thought. But she sensed that the detail itself was meaningless fluff. In fact, it was nothing more than babble. Was he hiding behind it? That was what it felt like, she sensed. It felt like a distraction. As if Trevor was intentionally tossing a different ball into the air, hoping they focused on that instead.

"Your conversations," she reminded him sternly.

Trevor didn't blink at the correction, but continued smoothly.

"So yes, there were a few occasions where I spent time with Isabella. There's a coffee shop in the center down the road, and my students know that it's open house – if they want to chat about anything, they choose a time and I buy! I think I had coffee with her twice. And she booked a couple of private lessons with me on the weekends. She was battling with her stamina, which is a very common issue. I was thrilled to have a one-on-one with her and take her personally through the exercises, making sure she had the right techniques and wouldn't injure herself as she strengthened."

"How long ago was that?" she asked.

"The first was a month or two ago, I think."

Stella glanced at Maxwell, wondering if he was also surprised by why Isabella would have battled with stamina at that stage, rather than at the beginning.

"Did she ever speak to you about her personal life, outside of the group classes?" she asked.

"Not to me," he said. He looked sorrowful, but he started blinking rapidly as he spoke. "I do maintain a very professional environment here, as I hope you can see. I don't have much social interaction with any of my clients."

"Really?" Stella asked. The blinking was a tell that he might be lying. And those intimate, caressing massages that Trevor Urban had been dispensing so generously after class hadn't looked professional to her.

"There isn't time, because the exercise is extremely intense. All-consuming, some of my clients have told me. I also offer general fitness, weight loss and diet advice if they request it, and we usually have those discussions at the coffee shop. But I keep from becoming personally involved beyond that."

His gaze pierced her. He had barely looked away from her since she'd walked in. In terms of body language, this was abnormal.

Stella agreed with the fact that these classes were intense. She could see that every person in that group had been utterly absorbed by the workout. And clearly, they all worshiped Trevor. However, she felt differently and didn't think he was being truthful. She thought that being in a high octane exercise program with a seriously hot instructor would spark a desire for closeness.

Trevor exhaled deeply. He sprayed the cloth and moved to the next bicycle, wiping it down carefully and thoroughly. Stella guessed this was a subtle indication that he had no more to say; and at that point, she couldn't think of anything else to ask.

However, she did not think that Trevor had told them everything he knew.

"Thank you so much for your help," she said.

"We may need to ask you further questions, or get more information from you," Maxwell added.

"By all means! Please, call at any time of the day or night. My business cards are on the desk in the lobby. Take one!"

Feeling bludgeoned by his charm, Stella turned away.

The room was very quiet. Glancing around, she saw that everyone had left. They headed out into the parking lot.

There were only two cars there. One was Maxwell's unmarked, and the other was a Porsche Cayenne SUV that must belong to Trevor.

This car was immaculately polished. And, thinking back to what Isabella's neighbor had told her earlier, Stella noted that it was bright carmine red.

"Trevor could have been the driver Isabella's neighbor saw," Stella said excitedly, pointing at the car. "I feel sure he was hiding something."

"I agree," Maxwell nodded. "He's false, and I didn't buy that whole charm offensive. But if he's hiding something, he's not going to tell us outright. We need to understand more about the whole dynamic of that class, and that means we need to move on to Isabella's friends, immediately."

CHAPTER TEN

Stella hastily programmed the GPS as Maxwell drove out of the studio and onto the main road. They were going directly from the studio to interview Barbs, who'd been the first of the two friends to answer when she called. Barbs had sounded eager to speak to them and had said she would be waiting for them at her home.

"I hope Barbs will be able to explain what really went on at Spirit Spin," Stella said.

"I didn't know what to make of that setup," Maxwell agreed. "I didn't feel Trevor was speaking to me, or even really noticing me, at all. You know, sometimes women feel they're invisible. I have had a few witnesses mention that to me but I never knew how it felt until now," he said thoughtfully.

Stella glanced at Maxwell, surprised by this insight.

"Agreed. He interacts with females. That's what he's been doing, and it's how he's built his career. Which seems to be going well. In a way, it felt more like a cult than a gym. With his looks and that very up-close-and-personal approach, it's like he's encouraging his clients to be physically drawn to him." Stella didn't voice her uneasy feeling that he'd also been assessing her in terms of net worth from the moment she walked in.

"It seemed very touchy-feely," Maxwell agreed.

"He drives a red Porsche SUV!" Stella couldn't let go of this fact. "Isabella's neighbor noticed a red SUV, and Trevor drives one. It's not that common a color."

Maxwell grimaced. "I know. I also want to latch onto that fact and not let go, but as Roth will remind us, we need more evidence. I also think the whole class dynamic is unexpected. It all feels – discordant, somehow. Like a minor chord in a major progression."

Stella was briefly sidetracked by Maxwell's use of words.

"Discordant? Do you play a musical instrument?"

She didn't know much about Maxwell. Had no idea of his passions and hobbies, other than that he'd been in a successful tech career before deciding to join the FBI.

He glanced at her in surprise.

"I play guitar. I used to stand in for the bass player in a local rock band, before I changed track and moved here," he said jokingly. "So yeah, discordant. That's how it struck me."

Stella was still trying to get her head around the short-haired, fit, terse Maxwell as a stand-in for a rock band, when they pulled up outside Barbs' house.

Barbs' home was in a well-established and scenic part of West Haven, Stella saw. They'd driven into a mini nature preserve, a wooded area with gracious beech and willow trees surrounding a lake. On this cloudy day the lapping waters were gray, but Stella could imagine that in summer it would be azure blue, with the waves reflecting the sun.

They tapped on the door, and a moment later, a young, dark-haired housemaid opened it.

"FBI Agents Maxwell and Fall," Maxwell said. "We called Barbara and she is expecting us."

"Please come this way," the maid said.

Stella glanced around in amazement as the maid proceeded down the wide, marble-tiled corridor and then into a glass-lined room with a magnificent view over the lake. Gray furniture and deep green plants accentuated the colors of nature outside, making the view feel seamless.

"Agents Maxwell and Fall are here, ma'am," the housemaid said formally.

Barbs was seated on the chair closest to the lake. She got up as soon as they entered, and hurried over.

Barbs was a petite woman with a cloud of platinum hair. She wore a strapless top and hot pants that accentuated a slim, toned figure that was all sinewy curves. Her face had strong, defined bone structure. She looked in her late twenties, but Stella guessed she might be a few years older.

"Please, sit. I am shattered by this. Shattered," Barbs said.

Barbs' words seemed to come from the heart and the gut. Without a doubt, she had been bludgeoned by the tragedy. Her large, dark eyes were swollen and red.

Stella felt immediate sympathy for her emotional state, but she reminded herself that until a suspect was arrested, nothing and nobody could be taken at face value.

"Please, tell me, who killed her? What happened? She was an angel!" Barbs continued anxiously.

Stella perched on the edge of a plush gray couch. The window glass was immaculately clean. The only marks on it were the tiny stars of misty rain starting to fall.

"We are trying to learn more about Isabella's life," Stella said. "Can you tell me more about her? How well did you know her?"

"Well, we used to see each other four or five times a week, at class. We'd occasionally go for coffee afterwards, but mostly we were training friends. She didn't have any enemies. There was literally nothing bad happening in her life that I know of. That's why I'm so shocked. This is just – it feels like I'm in a nightmare. Like I'll wake up and this won't have happened, because it couldn't have."

Barbs lifted her hands and pressed them briefly over her face. Her fingers were short and slender. Gold rings and bright jewels gleamed in the dull light.

"Nothing bad?" Maxwell asked, in suspicious tones. "Everyone has ups and downs in their life. This could be the result of something that seemed petty, but that escalated."

Barbs shook her head.

"She had a few moments. Her husband controlled her social life, which she sometimes got angry about, because she didn't have the chance to see her friends often. She did so well in the spin class, though. I think it became her life. She was a top achiever. Trevor praised her often, and used her as an example for the others. She was happy in class. And she didn't seem unhappy at home. Nobody's marriage is perfect, right? And Larry is quite famous, and definitely a good person. He's a leading businessman."

Barbs' tone showed Stella that she didn't think a leading businessman would ever commit any wrong. It was so much easier to place the blame for a crime on a person who didn't have power, status or wealth. Stella had learned that to her personal cost.

"Do you know why Trevor used Isabella as an example?" Maxwell asked.

"She worked really hard. Look, we all do. The classes are extremely motivating. And we're very competitive people. We're all go-getters, in our own ways," she further elaborated.

Stella wondered if there might have been another reason for the favoritism.

"What are your thoughts on Trevor?" she asked.

Barbs' face lit up. "He's a genius. Such a special person. He has such depths! He's so giving and generous, and of course, his classes are totally addictive. We live for them! He's very charismatic. I think he's created more than just a fitness class. It's an entirely different dimension to life. It gives us something very deep, on a spiritual level. Hence the name, Spirit Spin. We grow as individuals. We feel challenged. We feel alive."

She smiled. Her entire demeanor seemed more animated than it had been.

Stella's suspicions crystallized. Trevor had a psychological hold over his clients. With great power came the need for great responsibility, but Stella wasn't sure if that was part of the equation.

When you put a super-fit, super-attractive, ultra-charming and highly persuasive alpha male into a competitive environment with a group of ambitious and slightly dissatisfied women, things were not going to end well, she thought. And they hadn't.

Stella felt even more convinced that Trevor knew more than he had told.

"Thank you very much. Do you have Jasmine's number, by any chance?" Stella asked. "She also wasn't at class today."

"I'll send it through." Barbs grabbed her phone. "I don't know if she'll have any helpful information because like me, she only really knew Isabella from class. But maybe she can tell you more. I just want the killer to be found."

Barbs smiled sadly at them.

"Thank you for your time," Stella said, feeling that they had asked enough and that they weren't going to get any further information from Barbs.

She and Maxwell turned and headed out of the house.

"Roth messaged," Maxwell said, checking his phone. "He said Isabella's phone will probably be opened in the next few minutes. He suggested that we meet up at the local police precinct which is where the technician is working. If we hustle, we can get there by the time it's unlocked."

CHAPTER ELEVEN

Fifteen minutes later, Stella and Maxwell arrived at the Branford Police Department, which was handling Isabella's murder investigation.

Maxwell was clearly a regular here, because he barely had to show his badge before being greeted by the desk sergeant, and allowed entry to the back offices. In the third office down a long corridor, Roth was waiting. He'd set up his laptop and was using the screen to scroll through pages of data.

"Afternoon," he said, looking up and rubbing his fingers over his eyes, as if they were taking strain from looking at the bright, white surface.

"What's your feedback? Did you contact the gardener?" Maxwell asked. He took a seat on the other side of the desk, and Stella walked around to sit on the only other spare seat next to Roth.

"Yes, he's cleared. I got his home address and went past his house. He hasn't been home because he's been in the hospital. He fell off his bike on Monday night and broke his arm in three places. And smashed his phone, so he was unable to call in sick. He'd just arrived home after having the arm pinned. So, good news that he's not a suspect, but bad news that it's not that easy," Roth said. "Your side?"

"Stella has a theory that the spin class they all attended was really more of an exercise cult. There's something very strange about it, and they all seem to hero-worship the instructor," Maxwell said.

Stella felt pleased by Maxwell's strong support of her theory.

"Why do you think the cycle class is like a cult?" Roth asked Stella.

"The woman all seem hooked on it. The class itself was intensive exercise but it was also a compelling environment. Crazy loud music, low lights and lasers, and the way he took the class, it was an emotional experience, not just physical. And the instructor, Trevor Urban, got very up close and personal with his clients. Inappropriately so."

"Are we talking the kind of up close and personal that damages relationships and makes people act irrationally?" Roth asked thoughtfully.

"I felt the women who attended were hooked on him, as much as the exercise," Maxwell said.

"He said Isabella was just a client, but I suspect there was more to their relationship," Stella added.

Roth stared at her closely.

"You say this why?" he asked.

Stella felt frustrated by her inability to describe the intuitive feelings she had.

"There were pointers in his body language that he was lying. And, as soon as we mentioned Isabella, he took cover behind this wall of irrelevant information, which he presented with a lot of charm. Plus, he favored her in the sessions, and often used her as an example," she managed. It wasn't exactly what she'd wanted to say. Worse still, Roth didn't look convinced.

"It's good to know that Mr. Urban might be a marriage wrecker. Let's keep that top of mind as we go forward. We must now look for proof that confirms what we suspect."

Stella felt frustrated. If it had been up to her, she would have headed straight over to his house to question him again, and put the pressure on.

She wasn't sure how Trevor would respond to that. Probably, it would be pointless, she acknowledged. He was too slick, his persona too well controlled, for it to easily crack.

That meant she needed to think of a way to crack it, Stella told herself, staring around the small room with its bright white screen and bland, gray blinds. And that was why Roth was asking her for proof. Without evidence, questioning would be nothing more than words. Words which Trevor would expertly field. She remembered the cold intelligence in his gaze.

Evidence was needed in order to back up her intuition. How could she do it, Stella wondered.

At that moment, there was a tap on the door and a tall, lean young man walked in. He had sharp, intelligent features and a slight stoop to his shoulders that made Stella visualize him being hunched over a screen for hours at a stretch.

"Afternoon, Quinton," Roth said.

"Afternoon, Roth," Quinton replied. He nodded in a friendly way at Maxwell and Stella. "We've unlocked Mrs. Hartford's phone. I've written all the security details down for you here."

"That's great." Roth took the slim, silver phone carefully from him.

"I'm afraid there's not a lot of stuff on it. Which tells you something, I guess," Quinton said apologetically. "Messages were all erased. There are some recent calls and of course you can pull the call list. We might be able to get a copy of some of the messages but as you know, that will take time."

Stella felt frustrated by this. It showed that Isabella had been keeping information to herself. Something had been going on, that was for sure.

"Thanks for your work on it," Roth said.

The tech turned and walked out, rubbing his head thoughtfully as if he was already focusing on his next hacking job.

Eagerly, Stella and Maxwell peered over Roth's shoulder as he punched in the code to unlock the phone.

"Right, we do have some recent calls," Roth said, sounding pleased as he scrolled through the list. "I guess Isabella didn't have time to delete all of them."

"That means very recent?" Maxwell asked. Stella could hear the excitement in his voice.

"Yes, it does."

"Could be significant," Maxwell said again, and Stella felt encouraged that finally, they might have achieved a breakthrough.

"Here. Take a look." Roth showed them the screen.

Stella stared incredulously at the list.

"Eight missed calls? On the morning she died?"

"All cell numbers. Five from one number, then three from another. Her husband mentioned he called her a few times. Let's confirm which number is his, and check on the timing of those calls."

Quickly, Roth compared the numbers to his records.

"The calls at eight-fifty-five a.m., nine-forty-five a.m. and ten a.m. are from Larry's cell number. With the timeframe the coroner supplied, those were made after she was deceased. So now, we move to the five earlier calls," Roth said, scrolling back in the list.

"All from the same number," Maxwell said, his voice intense.

"All from the same cellphone," Roth agreed. "The first two were at seven-thirty a.m. Then another three, fifteen minutes later."

Stella felt her spine prickle. This couldn't be coincidence! Could it?

Someone had desperately been trying to contact Isabella. Either it had been the killer calling, or else someone trying to warn her, Stella thought uneasily.

“Let’s look up that number.” Roth turned to his screen and tapped keys. “Here we go, here we go,” he said impatiently.

Stella watched the screen, waiting for the information to refresh. This couldn’t happen fast enough for her. They were on the verge of a major breakthrough.

Then Roth let out a frustrated sigh. “Seriously? System’s hanging.”

“Again?” Maxwell asked incredulously.

“Third time this month, yes,” Roth said.

“Last time it was down for a whole day,” Maxwell said to Stella, now sounding angry.

Surely there was another way they could find the number, Stella thought, wondering what the solution would be. She knew that Roth would not allow them to call the number. Any call, no matter how innocent they made it sound, might give an advance warning to someone who could already be guilty and looking out for anything unusual.

Then Stella had an idea. A crazy leap of faith, but it couldn’t hurt to check.

She opened her purse and looked inside, finding the business card she had picked up earlier in the afternoon.

She stared from the numbers on the phone to the numbers on the card, unable to believe that her hunch had paid off. Shivers trailed down her spine. It was an exact match.

“You wanted evidence?” she asked. “This is the evidence. Right here. The person who tried to call Isabella five times early this morning was Trevor Urban.”

Finally, here was the proof that Roth had been seeking.

*

By the time Stella and Maxwell reached the Spirit Spin studio at five-thirty p.m., it was locked up. Classes were over for the day, but Stella had noted there was also a residential address on the card.

She felt extremely nervous as they turned in that direction. Trevor was such an unknown entity. His charming veneer was smooth and polished. He was highly practiced at assessing people, in the same way that a trickster or a fraudster or a street magician might pick up on body language.

He could well have been the killer, and might be violent.

“So, how about you?” Maxwell asked suddenly, interrupting her worried thoughts.

“What do you mean, what about me?” she asked, uncertain what he meant.

“Do you play a musical instrument?” Maxwell asked. “You see, you got that information from me. But I’ve decided it’s only fair that if you ask me something, I’m going to ask you, too.” He glanced at her with a mock-stern expression.

Stella surprised herself by laughing. She wondered whether Maxwell had sensed her nervousness and was trying to get both of them in a more relaxed frame of mind.

“I don’t play anything,” she admitted.

“Really? You’ve never wanted to try?” he questioned.

“I wanted to, when I was younger,” Stella admitted.

“But?” Maxwell asked.

“There was a piano at our school in Kansas, but I never got to play it because those lessons cost extra, and my mother couldn’t afford it. Piano wasn’t in the basic curriculum, but I used to be fascinated by it. When nobody was around I would sneak into the music room and pick up the lid, and press a few keys. I thought every single note sounded incredible, and filled with magic. I wished I could learn the skills I needed to make those polished keys sing. I longed for the ability to use those beautiful chords to create a story, a harmony. And as far as music goes, that’s the extent of my skill.”

Stella caught herself. She’d literally been right back there, in the schoolroom that smelled of wood and floor polish, pressing those keys. She could almost see herself – a lonely eleven-year-old girl in a faded dress, seeking comfort in dreams about the beauty of music, because the ugliness of her father’s loss was too much to bear.

Now Maxwell knew a lot about her, if he’d been listening perceptively, and Stella guessed he had been. She’d revealed more than she’d intended. He knew she’d grown up in Kansas and that she’d had dreams that were never realized due to lack of money, and that she’d only mentioned her mother, and not her father at all.

“Here’s Sunset Drive,” she said hurriedly, changing the subject as she saw the road name ahead and all her fears about the present rushed back.

It was apt, because the sun was moving below the clouds in a blaze of late afternoon light.

“This is the house,” Maxwell said in a low voice, as Stella took in the quaint yet modern, faux-colonial home that was set in a dramatic location at the top of the hill.

Maxwell parked on the sidewalk, behind a white Range Rover. The gate was unlocked. They stepped through, and headed up the paved drive to the front door.

Finally, they were going to question this man while armed with concrete and incriminating evidence. Stella wondered with a twist of her stomach what would happen during this confrontation.

Would they break through the charming, handsome façade, to discover a cold-eyed killer underneath?

As Maxwell was about to knock, Stella heard a faint but distinctive cry from inside.

She glanced anxiously at Maxwell. He looked back at her in concern.

“Did you hear that?” he muttered.

“Yes, I did,” Stella whispered. She didn’t dare to breathe, straining her ears to see if it sounded again. Had they misheard it, she wondered, starting to doubt herself. Had it come from somewhere nearby, or had it been the faraway call of a seagull?

The cry came again, louder this time. It was a woman’s voice, and definitely coming from inside.

Stella felt dread envelop her. What was happening in there? What if they had arrived too late to prevent a second murder?

On impulse, she tried the door, and was astonished when it moved smoothly open.

Maxwell reached for the holster of his service Glock. His movements were calm and competent. His training was clearly asserting itself over the fear he must surely be feeling. For the first time ever, Stella drew her own weapon and crept into the house behind him.

The door opened into a massive lounge which was empty. Stella assessed the space, keeping alert, watching every corner of the room, ready for any unexpected movement or threats. She kept aware of where Maxwell was as they listened for any sounds.

New money, Stella thought, as she looked around, her heart pounding in her throat. Everything in this home from the ultra-modern couches in the open-plan lounge, to the massive artworks of splattered color on the bright white walls, pointed to someone who had recently made it and was now splashing out.

Trevor had found his niche, and it had brought him riches, Stella thought.

Then her heart jumped into her throat as she sensed movement to her right.

She gasped, spinning around to face the threat, sensing Maxwell doing the same.

Letting out a shaky breath, Stella saw it was the curtain. The sea breeze was gusting in through the open window, causing the thick white fabric to billow out. That was all. There was nobody waiting to ambush them.

Then she inhaled sharply as she heard another scream, coming from behind the door at the back of the lounge.

Maxwell moved swiftly to the closed door with Stella close behind him.

"FBI!" Maxwell shouted, holding his gun at the ready.

He grabbed the door and flung it open before storming through.

CHAPTER TWELVE

Stella followed close behind Maxwell, moving to cover his left side as he barged into the room. But, as she took in the scene in front of her, she gasped in shock.

The cries were coming from the emperor-sized bed on the opposite wall. There, entwined on the pearly covers, were Trevor and Barbs.

Barbs?

Stella had only a moment to take in this impossible sight before the pair uncoupled. With a shriek, Barbs grabbed one of the silken sheets and pulled it over her, her dark eyes wide and horrified.

Trevor scrambled around to face them, breathing hard. He looked flabbergasted, his charm briefly abandoned. Stella didn't know where to look as she stared at him. Since he clearly wasn't holding a weapon, she kept her eyes firmly fixed on his face.

Almost as an afterthought, Trevor stood up. He grabbed an ebony bath sheet from the tiled floor, and fastened it round his waist, before speaking in irate tones that showed fury was rapidly gaining ascendance over shock.

"What is this? What the hell is this invasion of my privacy!" he half-shouted.

Maxwell holstered his weapon and stated calmly, "Mr. Urban, we need to question you again in connection with Isabella Hartford's murder."

Barbs gasped, staring at them in astonishment. Trevor was too angry to be in the least perturbed.

"You broke into my home at gunpoint to do that? I swear, you guys have been nothing but trouble from the time you barged your way into my business premises. Are you looking for a scapegoat, or what? There's a knocker on the front door," he added, sounding enraged.

Maxwell didn't twitch.

"We are in possession of new evidence," he said meaningfully. "After reviewing this evidence, we drove straight here to question you very urgently."

Although Maxwell hadn't even mentioned the call logs, Trevor had gotten the message. As far as possible under his deep sunbed tan, he was looking pale, and the anger had evaporated from his demeanor.

"Either we can forcefully arrest you as you are, or else you agree to come with us willingly. If you agree, you may get dressed first," Maxwell continued.

There was a pause. Stella guessed Trevor was examining his options and realizing that at this point he didn't have any. She saw emotions chase across his face. Resignation was the expression that finally settled there.

"I'll get dressed," he said.

If he'd thought the agents were going to step outside while he changed, Trevor realized he was wrong. She guessed Maxwell had taken note of the fact that the glass doors on the eastern wall led onto a balcony. He wasn't going to risk Trevor becoming a runner. Instead, he planted his feet in place. With a sigh, Trevor stood up, gathered some clothes from the wardrobe, and went into the bathroom.

Stella spent the time staring at Barbs, who stared back at her apprehensively.

"You didn't mention any of this when we questioned you earlier," Stella said curiously.

"I – I know. I should have done so. I really didn't think it relevant." Barbs looked embarrassed and apologetic.

"Now might be a good time to fill in the gaps," Stella suggested.

Barbs pulled the sheet even higher, so it covered all of her except her now frightened face.

"I don't think this is a good time," she said.

Stella felt otherwise. Barbs had lied to them once and if given the chance, she was sure she'd try to do so again. Now, while she was firmly on the back foot, was in fact the perfect time.

"Unfortunately, you don't have a choice in the matter," Stella told her firmly.

"All right. I will explain to you now, but please – in turn, can I ask you a favor? Please don't tell anyone. Please don't mention it to my husband, or let him know about it," she entreated.

At that moment, the bathroom door opened and Trevor walked out, fully clad all the way from his red dress shirt down to his shiny black shoes. He bent to pick up a leather jacket that was discarded near the bed.

"Let's go, Mr. Urban," Maxwell said.

"Give me two minutes," Stella said. "Barbs and I need to finish up. I'll meet you outside."

She turned back to Barbs. The front door closed and they were alone in the house together.

"I can't believe this is happening. Honestly, this has turned into a nightmare," Barbs said. Her eyes were full of tears once more. This time, Stella sensed self-pity was the overriding emotion, rather than the grief over her friend's death. Now, Stella was wondering all over again whether those tears had been fake.

She decided that it would be wisest to show some understanding for Barbs' entirely self-made predicament. She was sure she would realize there was now an unspoken contract between them; that providing honest information was the trade-off for not telling her husband.

"What you say will remain confidential," Stella reassured her. "And if you disclose everything now then there will be no need to re-interview you."

Barbs sighed. "I know I gave a false answer to your question earlier. I really am sorry about it now, but at the time I was just trying to protect myself, and I honestly didn't see why my relationship with Trevor was relevant."

"Okay," Stella said, understanding why Barbs had wanted to keep it a secret.

"Look, my husband is away a lot. He owns nightclubs, casinos, all sorts of places like that. I kind of assumed, when I found a few things out a while ago, that from time to time he probably ends up with one of the hostesses. I mean, he's a good man. A very good man, and a generous husband, but in his line of work I think it just sort of – happens."

She stared at Stella miserably, clutching the sheet tightly.

"It's okay," Stella reassured her. "Please carry on."

"Even so, I know that he wouldn't take it well if he found out I was doing the same. It would affect my marriage, and I have a nine-year-old daughter. Besides, what I have with Trevor is – well, it's not like an affair, really."

Stella felt surprised by this information. She'd thought it was exactly like an affair.

"How would you describe it?" she asked, hoping for clarity.

"What I have with Trevor is very special. It's not like anything I ever thought would happen in my life," Barbs confessed.

Stella noted the way her face brightened as she mentioned this. She felt puzzled all over again by the hold that this handsome instructor clearly exerted over his class.

"When did it start?" she asked.

"A few months ago, during one of our private evening sessions. I was battling so hard to get one of the moves right. He worked with me on it – it was so intense. I can't really explain how it felt when I achieved it. It was such an emotional experience. He was almost crying. Literally. Almost crying as he shared my journey with me."

"Is that so?" Stella asked, thinking Trevor was a better actor than she'd given him credit for.

"Then we just – he started kissing me. He was shaking. He said he'd never done this before. I said I hadn't either. The attraction between us was so intense. I will remember that moment for as long as I live," Barbs said in a voice taut with emotion.

Stella felt puzzled that Barbs had accepted these words at face value. Hadn't she wondered if he'd done such a thing before?

"And from then on?" she asked.

"Look, Trevor is a very compassionate person. He's pretty much a saint." Barbs stared at Stella intently. "I know it doesn't seem so to you right now, but you have no idea how caring he is. He told me he never, ever wants to put me at risk in any way. He said he would call things off if he thought that it would affect my marriage, but in the meantime – well, from time to time, we both can't help ourselves. After the trauma of today, he called me, and I headed straight here. We both needed comfort from each other. He was devastated about Isabella."

"Was that just because she was one of his clients? Or do you think he could have been romantically involved with her?" Stella asked carefully.

Barbs sighed impatiently.

"You are not understanding what I'm saying. Trevor is not a common cheater. He explained to me that he's never done this before and actually battled his own feelings for many weeks before he realized that he had no choice. And if he feels there's any risk to me, he will force himself to end it. But in the meantime, it's changed my life. He's so special to me, I even bought him a platinum medallion on a chain that he sometimes wears."

Stella felt incredulous at Barbs' single-minded insistence that she was having an affair with a saint. She hadn't even shown any curiosity about why she and Maxwell had arrived at Trevor's home, or demanded that he accompany them to the police station. She could clearly not conceive of her spin instructor being anything other than blameless.

Furthermore, the unclothed Trevor hadn't been wearing a platinum medallion on a chain when they burst in, but Stella had noticed a gold thumb ring with a large diamond inset. Suddenly, she wondered if that was another gift from a grateful 'I'm the only one.'

Barbs was so far in denial that Stella didn't think she would believe her if she provided actual proof that Trevor had been seeing other women. Although Stella strongly suspected this, she didn't have the necessary proof. Given that, she could now end this interview and allow Barbs to get dressed.

At least they'd proven Trevor to be a liar, which would be an advantage during the forthcoming questioning. More than ever, Stella was now certain that he and Isabella had been lovers and that something had gone wrong. Perhaps Isabella had found out she wasn't the only one and they had fought.

This interview was going to be critical. In fact, it could crack the case wide open, Stella thought, as she left Trevor's house and hurried to the car.

CHAPTER THIRTEEN

Thirty minutes later, Trevor was seated in an interview room at the Branford police precinct. Stella and Roth sat on the opposite side of the desk. Maxwell stood by the door, his arms folded.

Reading his body language, Stella was taken aback to see that Trevor didn't seem overly concerned about having been brought in. He'd recovered his seemingly impenetrable poise that was only briefly dented when he'd been discovered in flagrante.

His gaze moved thoughtfully between the three of them, but he didn't appear intimidated and was sitting at ease in his chair. He didn't even look worried by Roth, who was glaring at him and clearly bringing his toughest persona to this interview.

None of them had spoken since entering the room. This was a deliberate strategy when questioning a suspect. Silence made people uneasy. It created anxiety, and they would eventually seek to fill the vacuum by talking.

But Trevor seemed untroubled by the silence.

Eventually, Roth cleared his throat and began speaking. Trevor turned to him, listening calmly as he began.

"Mr. Urban, you were untruthful with us. You lied to federal agents. You said you had no close relationship with any of your clients. Clearly that is false. We have had new information come to light on Mrs. Hartford's call records. Information that is highly incriminating for you. You called her five times on the morning of her death, within the timeframe that she was murdered. So I am now giving you one last chance to tell the truth, and if you lie again there will be very serious consequences."

Again, Roth let a few moments of silence add extra weight to his words.

"What relationship did you have with the victim?" he asked.

Trevor stared at him, with a perplexed frown.

"You called Isabella repeatedly. Why was that?" Roth pressured.

Trevor shook his head. He looked genuinely puzzled, as if he was trying to make sense of a confusing and wrong account.

"You are correct in that I tried to call Isabella twice. It was a courtesy call, to confirm her bookings for the week, and whether she was joining the morning or afternoon class. I'm afraid that the other calls must have been pocket dials because I have no knowledge of them. I was busy setting up in my studio by then. My phone was in my pants pocket," he explained helpfully.

Stella seethed inwardly at this blatant lie, which despite being clearly false, was surprisingly difficult to counter. That was the problem with questioning an experienced liar who thought he had the upper hand.

"Really? You were in your studio? A neighbor saw a red car on the street, on the morning that Mrs. Hartford was killed. My theory is that you called her repeatedly, and when she didn't pick up, you drove to her home," Stella stated.

Trevor shook his head firmly.

"You are definitely on the wrong track. I don't even know where Isabella lives. Why would I visit her at home, anyway? We saw each other during class."

"Where were you this morning, between seven-thirty and nine a.m.?" Maxwell asked harshly.

"I finished the early class at seven-thirty. That was when I tried to call Isabella. Then I tidied up the studio, and left at about quarter past eight. I showered, changed, drove to the local shopping center and had breakfast at the café there."

"What's the name of the café?" Maxwell asked.

Trevor frowned, looking unsure for the first time. "Munch, I think. No, that's the one in the other center where I meet clients. I actually can't remember its name. But it's the place on the corner at the West Shore Center. There's only one café there, and a pizza restaurant."

"You ate alone?"

"Yes."

Stella thought this alibi sounded flimsy.

Clearly, so did Roth, who gazed cynically at Trevor.

"Prove to me that you didn't know where she lived," he said.

"Well, why don't you prove I did know?" Trevor said defensively.

"Don't your clients provide their address details when they register with you?" Stella asked. "Isn't that essential information for people doing an intensive exercise class where there's a risk of injury?"

She saw a flash of anger disrupt his controlled expression. She'd gotten under his skin, but only for a moment. He hesitated, but then resumed his charm offensive.

"Of course. Of course. Thank you for reminding me of that, Agent Fall. As I never make use of the personal information, I'd all but forgotten that their home address, next of kin, and medical insurance details are submitted on their records. The clients input all the data themselves. I'm a slow typist, even on an iPad, so it goes quicker that way." He smiled benignly.

"So you could have looked up Isabella's home address if she didn't answer your calls?"

"But why would I do that?" Trevor asked, sounding genuinely at a loss. "I was intending to call her later in the day. Clients are busy people. I don't know what you are trying to insinuate."

Of course he knew, Stella thought. He knew only too well and he was expertly evading it.

"You had an affair with Isabella Hartford," Maxwell thundered. The pitch of his voice made them all jump. Clearly, Maxwell was now using brutal shock tactics to break through Trevor's façade. "Give us the truth! It's completely obvious how you behave with your clients. Something went wrong between you. You called her multiple times, and then you arrived at her home. You fought, and you murdered her! Now admit to it!"

There was a ringing silence.

Trevor folded his arms. Sounding outraged, he retorted, "You are trying to coerce me into making a confession, simply because you want this crime solved. I agreed to be interviewed because I also want closure on my client's death, but I refuse to lie. I will not be bullied, or tricked, into admitting to something I didn't do. I demand to speak to my lawyer now."

Stella had the sense he was shutting down. She glanced at Roth, who stood up and pointed to the door. Stella and Maxwell followed him out and he closed the door behind him, leaving Trevor inside.

"I can't believe how he's lying!" Stella seethed. "He must have slept with her. It's completely obvious that there was something between them. You wouldn't go calling someone that many times simply to confirm if they were coming to class. Of course there was a bigger reason."

"I can't believe he came up with that pocket dial story," Maxwell muttered, sounding as frustrated as Stella felt.

"He needs to cool off for a while," Roth decided. "I say we leave him for half an hour or so. He can't call his lawyer. He's not yet under formal arrest. If we draw this out to the stage where he becomes uncomfortable and impatient, I think he'll get the message it's time to be honest."

They walked through to the small kitchenette at the end of the corridor. Stella was pleased to see a jug of hot coffee there. Maxwell got three cups out of the cupboard and Stella poured.

"Cream? Sugar?" she asked.

"Both," Maxwell and Roth chorused together.

"Two spoons, please," Maxwell said. "I need the sugar hit."

"It's been a frustrating session," Roth agreed.

"Lying to an FBI agent during a murder investigation is a serious matter. I can't believe he's continuing with it," Maxwell said incredulously as Stella passed him his cup.

She took a gulp of her own. Sweet and strong, she welcomed the sugar hit and the caffeine kick.

"I guess he's committed to that course of action now," she said. "And it seems to be his default, the same as he lies to his clients. He does it convincingly. Barbs thinks she's the only one," Stella agreed.

"He seems to have such a hold over them," Maxwell said.

"You can only have a hold like that over people if they want to be held. In a way, I think they have chosen to live in a fantasy world when it comes to Spirit Spin," Stella observed.

"Well, the one thing we do know now is that Trevor is a serial liar, who trots out false information convincingly in order to keep his business and reputation clean," Maxwell said. "That gives him a very strong motive for murder, and we're not choosing to live in his fantasy world."

Those words gave Stella an idea.

"I think I know what angle we can take when we go back in and question him again," she said. "If we can beat him at his own game, I think we'll get the truth out of him."

"And what's your plan for doing that?" Roth asked.

"Some serious misdirection, and creative bending of the truth. He won't expect it from us, and I think we can shock him with it. If he buys the story, he might just panic, and if he panics, we've got him. We just need to crack open his defenses," Stella said, as the idea for her plan of action crystallized.

Roth sighed. “We have one last chance. We can’t keep him much longer without laying formal charges. Go in again and give it your best shot, Fall, because time is running out.”

CHAPTER FOURTEEN

Stella opened the interview room door. Now that she was going to be face to face with Trevor, she felt extremely nervous about her idea. They were up against a very experienced liar who had a lucrative income stream to defend. Her bluff might not work at all, but she had to try.

"You two go in," Roth muttered. "I'll watch from the observation room."

Stella stepped inside, followed by Maxwell.

Trevor was leaning casually back on the plastic chair, with his hands loosely linked in front of him. He did look worryingly at ease, Stella thought. The psychological advantage she'd had just after discovering him with Barbs was now firmly in the past. He was regarding her with a half-smile.

"Mr. Urban. We have some more questions," Stella said.

"Please, go ahead." Now Trevor leaned forward, looking earnest. "I've already explained that I will help in any way I can. But I can't help in ways that are beyond my power. I really am an innocent victim in this situation and I feel that by keeping me here, you are wasting valuable time that you need to use to find the real killer."

Stella felt a surge of dislike for him. He was so false, so manipulative. And at heart, she suspected he was very different from the affable front he presented. She wished she could get to grips with who he really was. Trevor didn't just have a wall of charm, she decided. He had an entire fortification he was hiding behind.

"Thanks for the advice, Mr. Urban," Maxwell said, sounding irritable. "As soon as we are convinced you're telling the truth, we can release you. We're not yet at that point, and have more questions."

"Please, ask. Whatever they are, ask."

"Your relationship with Isabella. I need to know how close you were," Stella said.

Trevor gave her a sideways look. "We were coach and student. Absolutely nothing more."

"I interviewed Barbs," Stella said. "She was very insistent that she was the one and only lover in your life."

"Exactly," Trevor said, sounding triumphant.

"The problem is that you've already lied to us. So we can't take your word for it."

"What do you mean by that?"

"She mentioned she'd given you a medallion. But right now, I see you're wearing a ring. It looks expensive. Was that also a gift? Perhaps one of your other clients gave it to you?"

Now, Trevor's confidence was cracking, Stella saw.

"From – from a previous girlfriend," he stammered out.

"I recorded some of what Barbs said because I thought it was important," Stella told him. It wasn't actually true, but it sounded good.

"What was that?" he asked immediately.

"All about how you told her you'd never done this before, and that you'd call things off if you thought it would threaten her marriage. So, shall I tell you what we're going to do now, Mr. Urban, because I would like to give you one last chance?"

"What are you going to do?" he asked, now sounding seriously apprehensive.

"We got some other numbers of your clients from Barbs. We've collated a long list of them. We'll start by calling Jasmine, since she knew Isabella and Barbs well, and we'll continue from there. We're going to ask each and every one of them if they have a special relationship with you, or if they know of anyone who does. It might be that they all know nothing and that you are, in fact, telling the truth. But it may be that we will uncover some evidence of other affairs."

As she was speaking, Trevor stayed very still. He didn't seem relaxed any more, she noted.

"If we pick up hints that any others were intimate with you, I will play them the recording of the interview with Barbs," she continued firmly. "I wonder what they will think when they find out you cheated with her also? I wonder who else has assumed they were your only one and bought you expensive gifts? If you are lying, your reputation will be destroyed. Nobody will trust you, and you'll never do business in this state again. And it will all be your own fault, because you could have avoided it."

Finally, Stella saw with triumph that Trevor's veneer was cracking. The mention of the gifts had gotten him horrified. "Look, there's no need for that. No need at all. You guys – you don't have to destroy my business! My client information is privileged!"

"It's no longer privileged if the FBI needs access for a murder investigation," Maxwell threatened, taking the bluff forward. "We are going to pull your recent call records and messages from the past few months and scrutinize them. That will give us an even better idea of who to contact first."

Stella felt a thrill of satisfaction at Maxwell's additional leverage to her threat.

"No!" Trevor pleaded. "Don't pull my phone records. My clientele are from high profile families. If you go around deliberately causing trouble with them, I'm going to suffer the consequences."

Now he sounded genuinely afraid. Ultimately, she saw, it was his sharp business sense that was causing him to capitulate. Trevor wanted to protect his exercise empire at all costs.

"In that case, tell us the truth. And fast, because you've wasted enough of our time."

Stella was all out of patience with this cold-hearted user who had commercialized his charm. He had so much to lose. He'd just proved this to them.

"Please. This must remain confidential," Trevor implored.

"In as far as it can, being a murder investigation," Maxwell said.

Trevor sighed. "It's just part of what I do."

"What do you mean by that?" Maxwell asked.

"Honestly, it would be difficult not to get close to the clients, in such an intense environment. I realized quite soon that a lot of them wanted it. They were lonely or unsatisfied at home. It was, like, the full package for them. And I wanted it too, of course. I'm not saying it was a one-way street," he added hastily, glancing at Stella.

"So you basically sleep with most of your class?"

Trevor sighed. His shoulders slumped. Stella sensed he was abandoning his last attempts to withhold information and that, at last, they would learn the truth.

"I've slept with quite a few clients, yes. Not all of them, of course. But you'd be surprised how many are willing."

"Who instigates this? You, or them?" Stella asked.

"I do, if I pick up the vibes. Trust me, Agent Fall, those vibes are not subtle," Trevor said defensively. "And yes, they are generous. They give extra gifts. In terms of that, it's good business. But there's always the risk that their husbands will find out, and because of that, I don't allow the affairs to last long. I realized that early on. People get emotionally caught up. It can quickly become too serious and that's destructive."

Stella listened. It sounded as if Trevor had stumbled onto a lucrative and satisfying sideline to his business, which he had then milked to its full extent. She was interested to learn where Isabella had come into the picture.

"What's your average timeframe?"

"A couple of months. Some continue for longer than that. It's usually very easy to end it on a good footing. I explain that I need to step back, that the guilt is too great, that I cannot risk damaging their marriage, putting their children's future at risk."

Stella nodded. So Trevor had a neat technique for painting himself as the martyr. That allowed him to worm his way out of the relationship before it got too serious, as well as avoid any potential trouble.

"I tell them that we need to take a break. And I hint that at some future stage, I might not be able to stop myself from getting back together with them again. I think they like that. It flatters them, and makes them feel in control. I've had no disastrous outcomes so far. Until Isabella."

Now Stella leaned forward, feeling triumphant. Finally, they were going to get what they needed.

"So you started an affair with Isabella?"

"No!" Trevor practically shouted out the word. "If you have to believe one thing, please believe me when I tell you this. She came on to me, and I mean full-on, a couple of months ago. It was not the other way round."

"She really did?" Maxwell tested him, but Trevor now returned his gaze with more sureness.

"Yes. She was in a vulnerable phase of her life. She was looking for the excitement and spark that her marriage was not providing."

"And why was she so vulnerable?" Stella asked.

Trevor shook his head. "Her marriage was problematic. She complained that she was being controlled, that she had no voice, that she was distanced from her husband. The training sessions created a closeness which drew her to me," he said.

"Her husband is a high profile and well connected man. Did that bother you?" Stella questioned.

"Of course it did. I know her husband is a very prominent businessman who's politically connected. So I was hesitant, but in the end, I went along with it." He wrung his hands together. "It was easy.

She needed it. And she was a lovely, attractive woman. I mean, as a top model, she could have had any man she wanted. She told me she gets harassed by men all the time. On a continual basis. Being married doesn't make a difference. And she chose me. So, I admit, I was flattered."

"Then what happened?" Stella asked.

"I realized it was a mistake. She was very intense. Very demanding. She escalated things. I discovered she was a reckless woman. Things started getting more and more out of control. After a crazy episode between us this past Saturday, I called it off with her."

Trevor sank his head into his hands and rubbed his forehead.

Stella sensed that the confession was stressing him out, but that so far, he was remaining truthful. And importantly, Saturday was a recent timeframe. Things could easily have exploded as a result of Trevor's actions – or as a result of Isabella's response.

Maxwell then spoke, his words showing Stella he was on the same path. "What happened when you called it off?"

Trevor looked up, new lines of worry in his forehead now faintly visible.

"She lost it with me. She started screaming and flew into a huge rage. Of course, she was too hurt and offended to listen to reason, and she wouldn't believe me when I said I was concerned about her marriage. She said it was obvious that I didn't give a rat's ass about her marriage and that I was just trying to back out because I was scared."

"Where were you at the time?" Maxwell asked.

"We were at the studio. She'd booked a private Saturday morning class with me but it wasn't about the training, by then. She basically – we did it right there in the studio. On the platform. It was crazy, insane, beyond reckless. Afterwards, I told her as gently as possible that this had to stop. And she exploded."

"How did you react to that?" she asked.

"I kept trying to explain that the guilt was killing me, that if she had any compassion for me she'd call it off, that I respected her marriage. And then she began threatening me."

"Threatening you?"

"Yes. She became vindictive. She said that she was going to tell the whole class I'd cheated with her. I couldn't risk that. She threatened me just the same way you did! With destroying my business."

Trevor's voice was shaking with anger.

"Then what happened?"

"Then she stormed out. I didn't follow her. I was extremely upset and afraid. I decided to wait a while and see if she cooled off. I didn't want to wait, but I had no choice. She didn't attend class on Monday afternoon, so I decided I needed to call her and sort things out. I knew it might make things worse, but I was getting more and more worried that she was planning to do exactly what she'd threatened."

"So you called her?"

"I called her several times on Tuesday morning, yes. As the records show. She didn't pick up. So I then decided to leave it. I thought maybe she had decided to ghost me, and that she would now just disappear. I hoped she'd rethought things. I mean, Isabella had a good life. Why would she want to leave a billionaire?" Trevor asked plaintively.

But Maxwell shook his head. "The evidence against you tells a different version. And you have proved that you have no compunction about lying. I put it to you that you're lying to us once more. You decided to silence her permanently because of the damage it would do. You confronted her in her home gym. Perhaps you tried to pressure her not to talk, and she threatened you again? Then it was too much, and you snapped."

Stella watched Trevor closely as Maxwell spoke. If Maxwell's words hit home, she was sure that Trevor would show some subliminal signs that he was guilty. It would be very difficult not to.

But he didn't show any of the subtle tells she'd been expecting. Instead, he turned pleadingly to Stella.

"I swear I didn't kill her," Trevor implored. "I genuinely didn't know where she lived. I could have looked it up, but why would I? There's no way I would have gone around to her house. Why would I have done that? I had no idea of her setup, or who else would be there. It would have been a crazy move and I don't do crazy," he said firmly.

Stella exchanged a glance with Maxwell. She couldn't fault the logic in his explanation. The question was whether it was a true explanation.

It was time to pow-wow and see what Roth thought. They stepped outside the interview room where he was waiting.

"I don't trust his version," Roth said. "He had a very strong motive to kill her, and every opportunity. He could have gone to breakfast straight afterward."

Stella nodded. An ice cold person might have had the nerve to do that.

"We'll check it out, see if we can confirm his timing on that morning, but in the meantime, I'm arresting him on suspicion," Roth said. "With the amount of evidence against him, his confession to the affair and the break-up, and the calls that the morning, it's a strong case."

"Excellent," Maxwell said.

In a strange turn, Stella found herself the dissenting voice of the three. She'd been the one who suspected Trevor initially. But now, she found herself filled with doubt.

"Should we not rule out other possibilities?" she asked.

"Sure. We'll make the case as strong as possible," Roth agreed. "First thing tomorrow, we'll work on the timing. For now, you two can head home."

It was an order, not a question. Feeling frustrated, Stella walked reluctantly out of the police station.

She felt weighed down by the knowledge that if the real killer walked free, it would reflect badly on her. After all, she'd been specially co-opted onto the case. Even though she was here in a junior capacity they were still relying on her expertise, her background, and her intuition.

So what was her intuition telling her right now?

Trevor was an unethical person. He was a cheater, he took advantage, he misused his immense charm. But basically, Stella thought he couldn't have committed the murder because he was too smart. He wouldn't have done something as stupid and reckless as arrive at the home of one of his clients and murder her.

But somebody else had done exactly that.

With the up-close-and-personal nature of the crime, emotion had clearly played a key role. But what emotion had triggered such a violent action?

Stella realized that they'd missed out on a very important line of reasoning.

Trevor had been convinced that none of his clients knew about his doings, but Stella wasn't so sure. The women weren't stupid. Not all of them would be as deep in denial as Barbs.

Trevor had also been adamant that his clients bought the excuses he gave them when he broke it off.

Stella now doubted that, also. Isabella's own reaction had proved it. With such a high level of emotion invested in the class, of course some women would be hurt, humiliated and angry that he'd ended it.

Worse still, he'd then taken up with a beautiful woman, his chosen class favorite, a previous top model. Given all of the above, she reasoned, the motive for the crime could well have been jealousy.

CHAPTER FIFTEEN

Stella walked down the corridor to her new apartment. This was only the second night that she'd spent in the rental, on the fifth floor of a building near the outskirts of downtown New Haven. It might be small, but it was all hers, paid for by her actual salary as an FBI agent. In a way, her career shift still felt like a dream, she thought as she reached into her purse for the keys. And she'd never expected to spend her first working day involved in a murder investigation.

It had been a highly productive and hardworking day, where they'd gathered important evidence and made headway. At least, Stella tried to reassure herself that progress had been made. In fact, she wished she had more confidence that the suspect under arrest was the actual killer.

She fumbled with the keys, not yet automatically choosing the correct ones, and stepped inside.

The place was still sparsely furnished. She had a bed, a couch, a bookshelf, and a desk and office chair where she could set up her laptop if she needed to. The kitchen had a stove and a fridge. In the fridge were a few instant meals that she'd invested in. Cooking wasn't her forte.

She poured herself a glass of water, put a meal in the microwave, and paced around the kitchen, feeling impatient that she couldn't switch off from work mode the way she knew she should. Her mind was buzzing after everything that had happened today.

Who could she call, to share her fears and concerns about this case? Perhaps speaking to someone would help.

To her surprise, Maxwell was the first person she thought of. How good it would be to discuss her new theory with him. But, second-guessing herself, Stella reluctantly discarded the idea. She would feel self-conscious about calling him after-hours, especially when they'd been working together all day.

Her friend Rebecca, who she'd spoken to the previous day, was chasing a deadline tonight and working late at the office. But then, Stella thought of the best person of all. Her university mentor, Clem. After all, Clem had worked as an FBI special agent for decades. He would be able to give his experienced opinion on her theory.

The microwave pinged, and Stella took out her meal. Then, standing at the kitchen counter, she called Clem.

"Hey, Stella!" He answered almost immediately, sounding pleased to hear her. She imagined him, in his apartment overlooking the Chicago River. Probably, he'd be standing out on the balcony and, at this hour, opening a beer.

"How was your first day on the job?"

"Not what I expected at all," she admitted.

"Why's that?"

"I was making a start on some routine admin work, when a crime was called in, and they co-opted me onto the investigation team. It's a murder case."

Clem paused for a beat. "Would that be the Hartford case? I heard Larry Hartford's wife was murdered this morning."

Trust Clem to know about this already, Stella thought, impressed by how well networked he was.

"That's the one," she agreed.

"So you've been helping out today? Any results so far?"

"I need your advice. There's a suspect in custody. I initially thought he was the killer. He's not a nice man. I'd be very happy if I thought he was guilty, but now I feel he isn't, and that there was a different motive for the crime."

"You're using the word 'feel.' So you're going on intuition?" Clem asked.

Stella felt ashamed. "I know, I should search for evidence. That's what Roth keeps telling me. If I could work late tonight and find it, I would."

"The search for evidence begins with intuition. Don't forget that," Clem warned.

"I guess so," Stella acknowledged.

"The fact you have the intuition in the first place means that there are subliminal, or subtle, hints guiding you there. You're not just randomly deciding something. You're actually picking up on a variety of impressions – emotional, psychological, body language. And you are interpreting these to reach a conclusion. Remember, I went with you to a few of the interviews with criminals you did for your Master's thesis. I watched you work and that's what you do."

Stella felt better, knowing that Clem had such faith in her.

"So you think I must trust my intuition in that regard?"

“Absolutely. This is far from over. There are many, many cases where a suspect is arrested and subsequently released due to lack of evidence, or a case not being strong enough, or a better suspect being taken in. Roth must be under pressure to get results on this because Larry Hartford is politically connected. I assume that’s why the FBI is involved?”

“That’s correct,” Stella said admiringly.

“Having a suspect in custody takes the pressure off, for tonight, at least. It buys your team another day to examine the evidence.”

“Which I’m sure we’ll be doing,” Stella said.

“Ultimately, the evidence will lead you to the right person. That might be your current suspect. Or it might be someone else. So you keep listening to that intuition, Stella Fall. Pursue your theory. It’s why Roth wanted you on the case,” Clem advised.

“Thank you, Clem,” Stella said.

“Why do you think the suspect in custody is not guilty?” Clem asked, sounding curious.

“He’s false. He’s a cheat. He’s a serial liar. These are not our suspicions. They are facts we know beyond any doubt,” Stella explained.

“But?”

“He’s smart. He’s got a business brain. He’s very controlled. I think he’s too controlled to do such a thing. I don’t actually see him being stupid enough to expose himself that way. He’s told us himself he’s not stupid enough to do such a thing, and I believe him. If he did kill her, I think he’d do it differently and would put more planning into it,” Stella said, elaborating on her thought processes. “But yet – he’s so cold. So false. He hides behind a fortification of charm and I hate it!”

“You can always look into his background,” Clem suggested. “People build fortifications for a reason. Knowing that reason will help you to learn more about him, and that could give you added insight.”

“That’s a brilliant idea, Clem,” Stella said. “I’ll do that.”

She didn’t know anything about Trevor’s background. None of them had felt the need to ask. What Stella did know was that he didn’t appear to be a local boy. She had the strong impression he was from elsewhere, and had launched himself like a meteor into this society, shooting to success with his looks and charisma, and unique fitness class.

"My final advice is to keep trusting yourself. Don't you dare doubt your talents. They've got you to where you are, and they'll get you further," Clem then advised.

She felt relieved as she said goodbye to him. He shot from the hip, and always gave a brutally truthful opinion. If that was how he felt, Stella was confident she was on the right track.

As she took her steaming meal to eat on the couch, Stella remembered that she hadn't heard back from her mother. The message she'd sent her earlier, asking about her father, seemed like a lifetime ago. Her mother had had the whole day to answer, and she hadn't.

She checked her messages and stared down in confusion, because her mother's number didn't appear on her phone anymore.

Had she made a mistake? Stella searched again, this time with a growing sense of disbelief. There was only one possible reason for this, which was that Rhonda Fall had blocked her.

Feeling numb with shock, Stella tried calling the number, but it wouldn't connect. She'd been blocked on all sides – calls, messages. Her mother had read her plea this morning, and this was how she had responded.

Stella simply couldn't comprehend that her mother was acting with such hateful cowardice. For a moment she felt small and defeated all over again, back in the skin of her fearful, ten-year-old self.

Perhaps she should simply give up, she thought. Was it worth confronting the toxicity and conflict and barrage of lies? If Rhonda didn't want her to know the truth, she'd make sure Stella never knew it. She held all the power and was refusing to loosen her chokehold on it. Perhaps it wasn't worth the effort, and she should abandon the idea, try to forget about it, and move on.

And then a steely thread of determination tightened inside her. She was no longer ten, and no longer helpless. She had friends and connections that could help, she had the very best training in investigation and above all, she now had some hard-won confidence in herself.

Her father's disappearance had defined her life, and she deserved to find out what had happened, and why Rhonda Fall was trying to hide it.

But first, Stella reminded herself, she had to catch Isabella's real killer. If Isabella had been murdered by a jealous rival, she had to narrow down the possibilities of who it could have been.

Stella had one person in mind who she thought was most likely to know this information. Tomorrow morning, she was going to question her.

CHAPTER SIXTEEN

At eight a.m. the next morning, Stella pulled up outside a mansion set on a coastal road in New Haven.

She stared at the sweeping lines, the curved, gray-green walls, the clever multi-level building that seemed to be part of the hillside it was built on. This was the perfect home to create if you happened to be a leading architect, wanting to make a name for yourself for unique designs that stood out among the colonial, New England heritage.

Vincent van der Meulen was such an architect. He lived in this home, with his three children, and his beautiful wife, Helen.

It had taken Stella just ten minutes of research last night to confirm that Helen van der Meulen, the woman who'd first greeted them at the spin class, was the architect's wife. She had decided to pay her a surprise visit first thing this morning, and Roth had given her permission to investigate this new direction.

She'd decided to speak to Helen because Helen had mentioned that she was one of the longest-standing members of Spirit Spin. Therefore, she would probably know the most about the other clients, who had come and gone, what had played out over the past months, and if anything had seemed unusual in recent weeks.

Stella was alone this morning. Maxwell was following up on Trevor's alibi. That was urgent work, so she had to go solo. She was surprised by how much she missed Maxwell beside her, as she parked outside the artfully designed house.

As she walked up to the front door and rang the bell, she wondered what Maxwell would think of this setup. She knew he was put off by ostentatious dwellings and brash displays of wealth. She had a feeling he would like this house, though, and be charmed by how it nestled into the hillside as if it was a part of it.

"Is Mrs. van der Meulen there?" she spoke into the intercom. It's Special Agent Fall from the FBI. I need to ask some follow up questions regarding a recent crime."

A minute later, the front door opened, and Helen stood in the doorway.

The attractive, dark-haired woman was wearing skinny jeans and a designer T-shirt. She regarded Stella in dismay.

"You want to talk to me?"

"Yes, if it's convenient," Stella said firmly.

Helen spread her hands, looking stressed. "It is not at all convenient! This is one of our busiest mornings! We have children heading off to two different schools, and my husband is getting back from Berlin in an hour."

"I can come back later," Stella said reluctantly. "Or I could ride with you in the car," she then said, thinking of a better, and quicker, solution.

Faced with the prospect of having an FBI agent along for the car ride, Helen capitulated.

"You're here now and I did say the last time I saw you, that I'd be willing to help. So I'll try to juggle things. Please, come in. Take a seat in the lounge to your right."

The lounge was a glamorous room with dark leather furniture, pale gray walls, and bright paintings and cushions adding a splash of color. Stella noticed a discarded Barbie doll in the corner, and a stuffed dinosaur on the rug. The toys added a touch of homey-ness to this otherwise showpiece environment.

"Daisy!" she heard Helen yell. "Can you do both school runs? Yes, I know they might be a bit late!"

More shouted voices, and childish shrieks of excitement followed.

After the pandemonium had died down, Helen hurried back into the lounge.

"Right." She perched on a chair opposite the leather couch where Stella sat. "What can I do for you?"

This was really not an opportune moment, with family bustling around and her husband needing to be picked up so soon, Stella thought. But at least Helen had made time and was willing to talk. She hoped she'd be prepared to say enough.

Stella would have to word her questions carefully. Trevor had complied with the interrogation, in the end, so she didn't want to blow his misdoings out of the water. Hopefully if she asked her questions in the right way, Helen would talk without the need for that.

"This is a sensitive matter," she said in a quiet voice. "We have received confidential information on certain happenings, certain relationships and interactions, which have been ongoing at Spirit Spin. We suspect that these activities have something to do with Isabella

Hartford's death and that she was involved. I would like you to provide some background and tell me what you know."

Helen opened her mouth and closed it again, firmly. Seeing this inadvertent sign that she was closing up, Stella continued more forcefully.

"You willingly volunteered to help us with information. You told me you have been at Spirit Spin since it opened. I am sure you know what relationships I am talking about. Keep in mind that you are being officially questioned in a murder investigation, and that withholding facts may result in a felony charge."

Helen stared at her. For a moment, she looked absolutely furious and Stella feared that she might refuse the interview and physically throw her out.

Then her angry demeanor relaxed. She shrugged expressively. And, to Stella's surprise, she let out an amused laugh.

"I should have guessed you guys would find out about that," she admitted. "You are the FBI, after all."

Nodding calmly, Stella felt excitement thrumming inside her. Clearly, Helen was willing to talk, and was being honest.

"Can you clarify?" she asked.

"I guess you're talking about Trev getting close to clients? And in particular, to Isabella?"

"That's correct," Stella confirmed in a low voice.

Helen glanced around as a procession of three noisy children, an au pair, and another woman that Stella guessed was a housemaid, all clattered past the lounge and out of the front door.

"Look, let me say upfront, that Spirit Spin has absolutely changed my life. And I mean that in the most sincere way. After my youngest was born, I was forty pounds overweight. I felt terrible and my self-esteem was at an all-time low. Those classes were brutal. They destroyed me, but they worked. I could literally see the weight melting off me week by week, and Trevor was extremely knowledgeable and helpful about diet. He knew exactly what I should eat, as an overweight person wanting to get back to being slim and to do it sustainably. He was, and is, an absolute genius. He's a kind person. I know you probably think he's a criminal, but I don't," she said defensively.

"Thank you for the insight. Now, the relationships?" Stella said, gently drawing her back to the reason she was here.

"Okay. Well, I had booked a private session with Trev, and just as it ended, there was this moment between us. He'd been adjusting my posture. I was tired but felt on top of the world. We were both laughing about something. And then, boom, next thing you know, we were kissing."

"How long ago was this?"

"A few weeks after I started, I guess. I'd already lost a lot of the excess weight. So, as I said, there I was, feeling good about myself, and suddenly in a passionate clinch with this extremely handsome man who'd changed my life. I saw exactly what would happen next."

"And what did happen?" Stella asked, waiting for the inevitable confession.

Helen sighed. "I had this very unwanted epiphany. I suddenly thought – what the hell am I doing? Quite apart from the morals of the choice, I have three kids, I create my own art." She gestured to the colorful paintings on the wall which Stella now looked at in fresh admiration. "I have a crazy husband who wakes me up at three a.m. because he wants to discuss ideas about equally crazy buildings. I am a family woman, I've made my decisions in life, I am happy, and I do not have the time and energy for extramarital complications! I do not."

"Is that so?" Stella asked, surprised by Helen's admission.

"I hurriedly backed out of the situation, and we both looked at each other in a rather embarrassed way. And then Trev kind of shook himself, and carried on adjusting my shoulder posture. We finished the class and neither of us spoke about it again." She regarded Stella wryly. "I guess that didn't end the way you thought it would?"

"No, it didn't," Stella admitted.

But the fact Helen had asked that question in the first place told her something, she realized.

"Did you know he was doing the same with others?"

Helen looked at her sternly.

"I would really rather not name names," she warned. "If I tell you what was told to me in confidence, can you please accept it without needing other details?"

Stella thought quickly, and decided she had to accept this condition.

"I won't ask you for names," she promised, hoping she was doing the right thing.

"Well, a while after that, a friend and I were having wine together, and I told her what had happened. Then she admitted that he'd done the same, and had actually slept with her. She was quite pleased about it. Said it had been fun, and that she'd felt very complimented, and that he'd ended it at exactly the right time, before it started to become stressful."

"Anything else?" Stella asked, hoping Helen would say more.

Sure enough, after tapping her fingers on the arm of the chair for a few moments, she carried on.

"A month or two after that, we had a girls' night with a couple of other friends from class, and both of them admitted the same thing."

Stella felt intrigued. So some of the class had known exactly what Trevor was doing, and had shared it with others. And, interestingly, hadn't seemed to mind that he was sleeping his way around the class.

"Did you notice anything particular play out between him and Isabella?" Stella asked.

"When I saw he was using Isabella as an example, and paying her special attention in class, I assumed that they'd gotten together outside of class. I could see there was a spark between them, but like I said, it wasn't important to me and I really was there for the exercise."

"I understand," Stella said.

"I can't describe to you how the majority of us hero-worship Trevor. Including me, I must add," Helen elaborated. "My friends who had an affair with him all felt that it was a massive compliment, and that in a way it had improved their self-esteem, knowing this very handsome young man was irresistibly attracted to them. It was an adventure in their lives. When they realized they were all in the same boat, I don't even think any of them were particularly jealous. One friend even bought him a Rolex as a gift, because he'd made her feel desirable again," Helen explained.

There was that word again: jealous. The word that Stella now thought was the key in solving the case. In this weird environment, where Trevor had such a strong influence over his class, it had to have triggered an explosion.

"So nobody was upset?"

"No." Helen added, sounding more doubtful, "Well, none of my friends, at any rate. I'm obviously not sure about any of the others. I guess they could have been. Isabella could have been jealous if she'd found out she wasn't the only one, or someone could have been jealous of her. People are so different. We don't know everyone's situation, do we?"

That was true, because Isabella's reaction had been different. People were emotional, unpredictable beings.

"Can you think of anyone who seemed upset, who fought with Trevor or even with Isabella?" she asked, hoping that this would jog Helen's memory.

Ruefully, Helen shook her head. "Afraid not."

Suppressing her disappointment, Stella thought of another idea. "What about people who quit the class? Say, within the past couple of months? It seems like a popular class and there can't be that many people who left."

Helen rested her chin on her knuckles as she considered the question.

"You're right about that. Not many people quit Spirit Spin. There was someone called Abigail Mills. She was very enthusiastic about the classes and I remember feeling surprised when she suddenly stopped attending a couple of weeks ago. And Lauren – what was her last name? I can't remember her last name. Maybe I never knew it. But Lauren was also a good regular earlier this year and I haven't seen her around for a while now."

"Anyone else?" Stella asked.

"Yes, one other. I nearly forgot. Sarah Southey. Sarah attends morning classes. She hasn't been around for the past few weeks."

"Thank you so much," Stella said.

She stood up, not wanting to take any more of Helen's time. This had been an extremely productive interview and Stella now had a brand new direction. The more she thought about it, the surer she became that jealousy was the motivation for this crime.

She was going to question all the women who had surprisingly quit such an addictive and compelling class. She was going to ask then why they had done such a thing and what they knew. And, most importantly, where they had been on the morning Isabella Hartford was murdered.

CHAPTER SEVENTEEN

An hour later, Stella met Maxwell outside the doors of Spirit Spin, where a detective from the Branford precinct was already waiting.

"Good morning," the detective said, as he and Maxwell climbed out of their unmarked vehicles and headed to the door. "The warrant is organized, and Mr. Urban handed over the keys to us willingly. We're fully authorized to search the premises and access information."

"Thank you for organizing everything," Stella said politely. "And thanks for being here, Maxwell." Since she was accessing Trevor's client records, she'd asked him to come along in case there were any IT issues or unexpected hitches that needed his expertise.

Maxwell pushed his shades on top of his head. Stella thought he looked tired and frustrated, but he managed a quick grin.

"Hopefully it's hassle-free. If not, it's always interesting to have an IT challenge," he said.

"You two go on in. I'll wait outside," the detective said. "There have already been a couple of clients arriving, and I don't want anyone interrupting you," he explained.

Stella guessed Trevor's sudden arrest had not given him time to notify all his clients, so word hadn't filtered out to the entire class. She headed up to the main door and pushed it open, hoping that she would be able to find the information she needed.

The exercise hall looked dark and gloomy, thanks to the thick blackout blinds that were necessary to create the immersive environment. There was a row of light switches the wall near the door. She snapped them all on.

The lights flickered into life, and in a moment the room was brilliantly lit and looked like a spin bike showroom, but without the nightclub atmosphere she remembered. What a difference the colored lights and sound system made.

Staring around at the numbers of bikes, the immaculate flooring, and then up at the roof where the lasers and strobes were mounted on beams, Stella was impressed all over again by the scale of Spirit Spin in size, as well as luxury. Even the row of lockers along the right hand wall had doors made of polished wood and gold numbers. Trevor really had invested everything into his business. That made her more certain that her intuition of yesterday was correct. Surely Trevor could not have acted so recklessly to 'protect' his empire by committing a crime that would almost certainly destroy it.

At the end of the lockers, a doorway led into the changing room and showers, and on the opposite side of the room was another door that must connect with the back office. That would be where the records were kept.

"Let's go and see," Stella said, heading across the room to the door and pushing it open.

To her surprise – or perhaps not, Stella revised, an office was not, in fact, the main function of this large room. It contained an enormous, sumptuously cushioned couch, an elegant and extra wide chaise-longue, and there was a large, framed mirror on the opposite wall. An archway led through to a walk-in rain shower that was more than big enough for two.

The mahogany desk on the right hand side of the room, with its angular office chairs, was the only token gesture toward business.

The silver laptop on the desk was closed. Maxwell opened it and keyed in the pass code that Trevor had supplied. Stella waited anxiously to see if it worked. To her relief, the computer screen refreshed and he was in. That was good. She felt impatient and didn't want delays.

"So, what are we looking up?" he asked.

"Abigail Mills is the first of the clients. We need her contact details," Stella said, feeling excitement and resolve tighten her stomach as she thought about her theory.

"Okay. Here you go. Old-fashioned printing probably quickest?" he suggested.

Stella leaned forward as the record flashed onto the screen. There were Abigail's details. The printer thrummed, and Maxwell handed her the page.

"The next one is Sarah Southey," she said.

A moment later, that page slid cleanly out of the printer.

"The final one I only have a first name for," Stella said. "Lauren."

Maxwell frowned down at the screen, tapping his fingers on the desk. "There are two Laurens in the records. I guess you'll have to take both and do a process of elimination. Unless there's another way."

Drumming his fingers faster, he scrutinized the records.

"Okay, so some clients have the monthly membership. That means that for an extortionate fee, they can attend class whenever they want. The majority of the clients are on that plan. But a few are on the once-weekly lesson plan and Lauren Briggs was one of those."

"What does that mean?" Stella asked.

"It looks like she did the Monday classes at six-thirty a.m. Including this past Monday. So she is still current, according to the books. Therefore, it's the other Lauren you need. Her name's Lauren Healy."

"Thanks," Stella said gratefully as the final page was printed.

"Let me check the records, and see if there are any others who've quit recently. There might be more you weren't told about."

Maxwell scrolled through.

"No. None that I can see. Everyone else seems fully up to date."

Exiting the client list, he tapped the keyboard again with an intent look on his face.

"What are you doing now?" Stella asked.

"This computer saves footage from the security cameras outside the building. I'm accessing that now," he said.

Stella understood. Hopefully, by viewing this, Maxwell could build a timeline of Trevor's activities on the morning of the murder. Having an exact departure time from Spirit Spin would be essential, she realized.

"Here we are." Quickly, Maxwell scrolled back through the footage.

"So, Mr. Urban departed Spirit Spin at exactly eight a.m. yesterday morning." He checked his phone, swiping through his apps, and Stella guessed he was researching how long it would take to drive to Isabella's home in Branford.

In peak morning traffic, Stella guessed the drive would have taken about twenty minutes. Trevor could have done it, but then he would not have arrived at the local café where he said he'd gone for breakfast, until a quarter to nine.

That narrowed the timeframe, which Maxwell could now confirm with the restaurant. If he'd arrived at a quarter to nine or later, he could have committed the murder. If he'd arrived earlier than that, then the timing cleared him.

It was fascinating how the timelines slotted together to form such an important piece of the puzzle, she thought. She was starting to understand Roth's intense preoccupation with the evidence above all else. Evidence didn't lie. People, on the other hand – well, Stella was beginning to think they did nothing else.

"Can the café confirm the time he arrived?" she asked.

Maxwell shrugged, and Stella guessed this was why he'd been having a frustrating morning.

"The owner's out of town, and back at lunch time. He's the only one with access to the camera footage. And the waitresses who were on duty Tuesday morning, are both off this morning, and have to be specially called in."

"In that case, do you want to come with me?" she asked.

Maxwell brightened at the suggestion. Then, reluctantly, he shook his head.

"I have to be there when the waitresses arrive. We need this information as fast as possible. I hope your interviews get results. I'd rather be going with you."

His tone showed exactly how much he enjoyed waiting.

They walked out of the office and Stella switched off the lights, plunging the place once again into gloom.

Outside, the hazy morning seemed bright by comparison. Two women had arrived in SUVs. Both were slim, attractive, dressed for class, and were talking anxiously to the police detective.

"Has there been a crime here?" the first woman asked, glancing at her friend.

"Is Trevor okay?" the friend asked, sounding even more worried.

Listening to their tone, Stella wondered what relationship these two women had enjoyed with their handsome instructor. Given the odds, the chances were that they had been intimate, but now was not the time to ask.

"He's been detained following a murder," the detective answered shortly.

"Yes, yes, the murder. So shocking! We heard about that, of course. I remember Isabella from class. She was such a beautiful woman."

The other woman nodded. "I remember actually speaking to her. It's so tragic. I'm glad Trevor is helping the police." She paused, as if taking in the policeman's words. "Wait a sec. Trevor isn't under suspicion for this, is he?" she asked the detective with a note of righteous anger in her voice.

"Ma'am, you'd need to speak to the investigating officer in charge. Please ask for Detective Benjamin at the Branford precinct, and he'll update you on everything that we're permitted to share."

Clearly, this detective had decided it was wiser not to get into an argument with the two irate clients, and Stella couldn't blame him.

"Detective Benjamin. I will do that."

The women trailed back to their expensive vehicles and as they went, Stella overhead their conversation, delivered in piercing and annoyed voices.

"They believe Trevor was guilty in some way!" one said to the other incredulously. "I feel like we're living in a police state! I mean, how insane is that?"

"I don't know what 'detained' actually means. Is it the same as being arrested? Do you know?"

"I'm also not sure but it doesn't sound good. When my sons get detention it means they've done something bad, right?"

"It might just mean he's helping them with information, or they have to check his alibi, or something," the other said. "Shall we go and run around the track at the country club?"

They climbed into their cars.

Maxwell shook his head in disbelief. Stella knew that, like her, he was puzzled all over again by the sheer extent to which Trevor could do no wrong in his clients' eyes.

But not all of his clients had been so unwilling to find fault, Stella reminded herself. Isabella had flown into a fury over Trevor's actions. She was sure that among the three clients on her list who had so suddenly quit class, she would find equally destructive emotions in play.

If her intuition was correct, there was a strong chance this list would lead her to the killer. Climbing into her car, she set off to find out.

CHAPTER EIGHTEEN

The closest client to the spin studio, geographically, was Sarah Southey, whose address was in neighboring Milford. Stella called her while she was on the way to her home.

Sarah answered almost immediately.

"It's Agent Stella Fall from the FBI. Mrs. Southey, I need to interview you for background information in a murder investigation," Stella said.

There was a surprised silence.

"You want to interview me?" Sarah said, sounding surprised. "I'm not even a client at that place anymore."

"Why did you leave?" Stella asked. "Ma'am, we need to speak face to face." She checked her map. Five minutes, and she'd be there.

"I don't think we'll be able to speak face to face," Sarah said reluctantly.

"Why's that?"

"I left because we moved," Sarah said, sounding anxious. "We relocated three weeks ago and I'm now living in Charleston. I only saw Isabella a couple of times. I wouldn't remember her at all except Trevor used her as an example in the class once or twice."

"Thank you so much for the update, and for your time," Stella said.

Pulling over, she rerouted her GPS with a sigh, trying not to think about the fact that this was the first strike. Three strikes, and her theory would be out of the window. She decided to call the next one on the list, Lauren Healy, before driving to her home in Madison, New Haven.

Lauren's phone rang and rang. Stella thought it was going to ring through to voicemail, but at the last possible moment she picked up. She sounded as if she was somewhere busy. There was a lot of background noise and voices.

"Hello?" she said. "Hello, Lauren here."

"It's Agent Fall from the FBI. I need to speak to you regarding the recent murder," Stella said.

"Why?" The woman's voice was instantly sharp with suspicion, which in turn got all Stella's instincts prickling.

"Just routine questioning. We're looking to check some facts."

"I don't attend that class anymore. I'm no longer a member there."

Thinking quickly, Stella decided to try a different approach.

"Ma'am, as long as you were at class within the past couple of months, and saw the victim at least once, your account can still be helpful," Stella said.

Lauren sighed impatiently, as if acknowledging that Stella was not going to give up.

"I'm at breakfast at Patti's Place Country Estate. We're about to finish up, but if you're on the way, I can wait for you."

Quickly, Stella checked her maps to see how long it would take.

"I'll be there in ten minutes," she said.

*

Patti's Place Country Estate proved to be a garden restaurant attached to a beauty salon and spa. The wood-fronted, lodge-like building was set on a large estate amid perfectly mown and well treed grounds. It felt like somewhere you'd go on an expensive vacation, Stella thought, as she climbed out of the unmarked and headed straight for the restaurant entrance to the right of the spa.

At quarter to ten in the morning, about half the tables were still occupied by people finishing off their breakfast. All of them were in pairs or in groups except one, Stella saw. The woman sitting alone looked expectantly at Stella when she walked in.

She headed straight over, aware that this pretty, curly-haired brunette represented one of her two remaining chances. She mustn't blow it. She needed to ask the right questions, and do so in a way that would encourage the defensive Lauren to relax and open up.

"Morning. Are you Lauren Healy?" she asked with a quick smile.

"I am."

The table for four had been mostly cleared and a waitress was removing the last empty plates and cups. Stella sat down to her right.

"I'm Agent Fall. Thank you for waiting for me. I appreciate your help with this investigation."

Lauren frowned. "I am still not sure how I can help. I mean, what exactly do you want to know?" she asked. She sounded suspicious and prickly.

Stella wondered if the past ten minutes of waiting had given Lauren time to think about what she might, in fact, want to know, and to regret agreeing to speak to her.

"We're looking for some background on the spin classes that Isabella attended before her death."

"Why's that?" Lauren asked. "Is there a problem with the class? I mean, how is this all relevant?"

"We need to gather as many facts as we can, so we are checking background information," Stella said, deciding to take a leaf out of the detective's book by disclosing as little as possible. If Lauren didn't already know about Trevor's arrest, the information would spook her further, and make her even less eager to talk.

"When did you start at Spirit Spin?" Stella decided to lead in with the easy questions.

"I started at the beginning of the year. New Year's resolution," Lauren explained, with a sour smile.

"And you said you left a month ago?"

"I did, yes."

"What was the reason for that?"

Lauren shrugged. "I was busy. My daughter's sports started conflicting with the spin times."

Those weren't great reasons. Stella was not convinced by them. It would have been easy enough to cut down on the classes, or attend at a different time. But instead, here she was at breakfast.

Stella had the clear impression that if she was pressured too hard, Lauren would either shut down completely or explode. For now, the only course of action was to continue questioning her gently, even if it felt like walking a precarious tightrope.

"Were you disappointed with the classes in any way?" Stella asked.

Lauren shook her head. "I told you why I left. I don't understand why you're asking me this."

"I'm trying to get a clear picture of them."

"Well, I've basically told you all I know," Lauren retorted.

"What about the instructor, Trevor? What did you think of him personally?" Stella watched Lauren carefully as she said his name. Her face tightened briefly.

Lauren stared at Stella with narrowed eyes. "I don't have an opinion on him. Like I said, I stopped the classes because I'm very busy."

Stella was now up against a barrier of defensiveness. The only way to break through now would be to push Lauren further.

"Tell me about your relationship with Trevor while you attended the classes," she asked.

Her fears about the explosion were realized. Lauren gulped in an angry breath and, scowling furiously at Stella, let her have it.

"What exactly are you insinuating with this line of questioning?" she said in a high, furious voice.

"Ma'am, I –" Stella began, but couldn't stem her angry tirade.

"I can see exactly what you are implying, and it's disgusting! I did not agree to be humiliated by you, and to have my name brought into disrepute and my morals questioned. It is not relevant to me in any way, and I do not agree to continue with this interview! This was a fitness class! Nothing more!"

Her face had turned bright scarlet, physically confirming the truth of the relationship that she was verbally denying.

Stella needed to control the situation, urgently. She would get no further with this line of questioning. Lauren was not going to admit to what she'd done. But her loud retaliation was drawing attention. People at the surrounding tables were glancing their way, looking worried. Worse still, the restaurant manager had noticed. The young man, dressed in a smart black suit, was heading to their table with an officious look on his face.

Even though confirming the relationship was now a dead-end, Stella still had to check Lauren's alibi. She stood up and faced the manager, hoping to get her say in first. She could not allow Lauren's guilty ranting to cut the interview short before she'd found out where she was at the time of the murder.

"Good morning, sir," she greeted him and showed her badge. Then, in a low voice, she added, "Agent Fall from the FBI. I'm confirming details on the recent murder. It's unfortunately an upsetting discussion for Mrs. Healy."

"I want her gone!" Lauren seethed to him.

"I'll be one minute. We're almost done," Stella pleaded.

"Please, no longer than a minute, ma'am. This is disturbing our other patrons," the manager said sternly, before turning away.

The mention of one minute had allowed Lauren to get a lid on her guilt and anger and she'd now lapsed into smoldering silence. Quickly, Stella sat down.

"Were you in the Branford area at all yesterday morning?" she asked, getting to the point as fast as possible.

Lauren shook her head firmly. "My daughter was ill yesterday morning with stomach flu. I took her to the medical center in Westbrook. We had an appointment with Doctor Steel at eight a.m."

"Thank you for this information, and for your time," Stella said, jotting down these details to check. She got up and walked out as fast as possible, disappointed that the interview had yielded nothing more conclusive than an alibi.

Abigail Mills was the only other cancelation in the group. This was Stella's last chance to prove her theory right.

Everything hinged on this next interview.

CHAPTER NINETEEN

Stella was intrigued to see that Abigail Mills' home address was a grand mansion that was in a neighboring suburb to Isabella's home, and only about ten minutes' drive away.

Abigail was home and waiting at the door. She'd sounded taken aback when Stella had called, but had agreed instantly to be interviewed. She was tall, very slender, and very pretty, with tawny brown hair cascading over her shoulders, and sparkling green eyes. Immediately, Stella pegged her as somebody who would have been likely to catch Trevor's eye. She resolved that she was not going to allow Abigail to lie about the relationship. Whatever it took, however much of an explosion it triggered, she would have to pressure her to spill the truth.

"Come in, come in." Turning, Abigail led the way into a lounge that was decorated in green and blue to echo the sea views that were visible through the large French doors. A housemaid was busy tidying away some scattered toys that were lying on the sumptuous, sea-green rug, packing them into a large laundry basket.

She nodded politely before turning and carrying the toy basket out.

"Please, sit, sit." Abigail sat down on one of the couches.

Stella wondered if repeating her words was a nervous glitch. Abigail seemed unsure of herself. She wasn't as self-confident as Lauren had been.

"You said you want to know about the spin classes?"

"That's correct, Mrs. Mills."

Abigail thought about the question for a minute, twisting her fingers together.

"I'm not sure why you're asking me, as I quit recently," she then confided in Stella.

"Did you quit very recently?" Stella asked. She recalled Helen had mentioned that she hadn't seen her for a couple of weeks.

"Yes. I enjoyed the classes, but I ended up with too many other commitments, sadly," Abigail said with a regretful smile.

She was giving a reason right off the bat. Stella wondered how truthful it was.

"How long were you there?"

"Since June. I actually joined to lose weight for our summer vacation in August. My husband encouraged me to join. He owns the Health Emporium stores and website, so image is very important to both of us," Abigail explained. "Then I continued with the classes to deal with the weight I gained after vacation. It's an ongoing challenge," she explained with another quick smile.

Stella couldn't identify so much as an extra pound on her slender build. If Abigail had told her she'd quit the classes because they were making her too thin, it would have sounded like a more plausible excuse.

"Were you friendly with Isabella?"

Abigail raised her eyes to the bright turquoise seascape on the opposite wall while considering this question.

"Yes, I do know her. My eldest attends the model classes she ran at the arts school. And our family supports a few of the charities she's involved with, so we've spoken to her from time to time at events."

Stella paused. It was significant that Abigail knew Isabella and had interacted with her previously. Now, it was time for the challenging questions.

"Was Isabella friendly with the others in the class?" she asked.

"Oh, yes. She was a friendly person. Charming. Always had a smile," Abigail said.

"What about her relationship with Trevor? I understand he used her as an example often. Do you know if they were close outside of class?"

Immediately, Abigail's gaze slid sideways.

"I can't really comment on that."

"Why?" Stella pressured.

Abigail gave an uneasy laugh. "I was only there for exercise. I have no idea if they socialized outside of class or not."

She was now fidgeting with the corner of the blue and white scatter cushion beside her. Her fingers were worrying at the satin fabric. Stella didn't think she was even aware she was doing it.

"What was your impression of Trevor himself?" she then asked.

"Very knowledgeable. A good coach."

Her cheeks were suddenly more blush than alabaster.

Every single sign Abigail gave was pointing to the fact she and Trevor had an affair. Plus, she lived in Isabella's area, she knew her well, and Abigail was clearly concerned about her own looks and image, which could have triggered an emotional storm if she'd been dumped for an ex-model. The last few days could have caused a cascade of events, Stella thought.

How could she pressure the truth from her?

She decided shock value would be the way to go. Up until now, she'd been asking routine questions in a calm way. They'd developed a rhythm. Even though the tangent was making Abigail uneasy, she'd clearly decided she could handle it, that these evasive and flimsy answers were satisfying Stella while keeping her firmly out of trouble.

It was time to stir things up. In a breath, Stella needed to turn into an aggressive, terrifying person who would jolt Abigail all the way out of the comfort zone she was hiding in.

She drew herself taller and sat square, narrowing her eyes with a hard expression as she scrutinized her. Abigail blinked, surprised by the sudden change in body language.

"Mrs. Mills, you've been wasting a federal agent's time with these answers," she lashed out at her in the most vicious tone she could summon up. "I didn't come here to listen to your lies and your ridiculous half-truths. Do you think I'm stupid? A woman has died, and you're withholding information. I don't have time for this nonsense, so I'm going to bring you in to the New Haven field office. Come with me to the car. Let's see if a few hours in an interview room can get some honesty out of you."

She stood up decisively.

Abigail uttered an audible gasp. It was as if Stella had punched the breath right out of her. She stared up at her in utter shock, blinking even more rapidly.

"I – how dare you call me a liar? I've been cooperating as best I can," she tried in a breathy, wavering voice. Then she added, weakly, "Please don't bring me in. I'm so busy and it will be difficult to explain."

Relentlessly, Stella continued. "Then tell me the truth. This is your last chance."

For a few more seconds, she held her gaze until Abigail looked down. She was breathing hard.

"Okay. Okay," she said weakly.

Stella sat down again. "You had an affair with Trevor. Don't ask me how I know. I'm not asking you. I'm telling you. All you need to do is nod to confirm it."

Abigail's face was now a sullen scarlet and her mouth was twitching.

She stared at the floor a while longer. Finally, she gave a reluctant nod.

"Now, give me the details," Stella pressured her.

"Please, nobody else must know," Abigail muttered.

"It's only you and me in the room," Stella assured her.

"Alright," Abigail gasped out suddenly. "Here's the truth. I had a fling with him. He basically, like, seduced me and dumped me. I was hurt and angry and that's why I quit the class."

Stella felt massively relieved that her approach had worked. Now, while Abigail was talking, she needed to capitalize on it, and see how much more she could get.

"When did this happen?"

Abigail shrugged, looking angry and embarrassed. "About three weeks ago."

"How did it play out?" Stella asked. Now that Abigail was talking, she'd toned her approach all the way back down to conversational. Hopefully with the main confession now on the table, Abigail would be prepared to fill in the details. In the process, she might even trap herself into mentioning the crime.

"It was very intense, but I guess Trevor had been building up to it, so it wasn't out of the blue. He'd been flirting and – well, I was in that vulnerable place where I flirted back. Then it happened and I – I didn't know what to think. It was crazy. It was like nothing I'd ever expected to happen in my life."

"How long did it last?" Stella asked.

"It only happened once. I was so confused. First he was all over me, telling me that he'd never done this before but that I was irresistible to him. So I fell for it. I went home with him after a private class. I knew it wasn't going to be a long-term thing. But I definitely didn't expect that he would basically dump me afterwards."

"What did he say?" Stella asked.

"He said he couldn't bring himself to carry on with it, and he was worried about my marriage!" She sounded livid. "He started messing with my head. I mean, where was his worry when he seduced me? I got the impression he'd just been looking for a trophy and I felt so used. If I could have turned back time, I would have said no."

"So is that when you quit the class?" Stella then questioned.

"I quit," Abigail confirmed. "I decided I wasn't going to go back. I mean, he's not the only coach in the world. There are plenty of other options," she said angrily.

"Did you notice him flirting with anyone else?"

"He flirts with everyone," Abigail said bitterly.

She felt encouraged that they had gotten this far in the account. But in order to have a motive for the crime, Abigail had to have known that Trevor had turned his attentions to Isabella. How had that happened, she wondered.

"Did you see Trevor again, or get in touch with him to say you were quitting?" Stella asked.

"I didn't," Abigail said. There was an emphasis on the word 'I' that intrigued Stella. Hoping that silence would create a vacuum that Abigail would seek to fill with further explanation, she simply waited.

"I decided I was never going to speak to him again. But then, a week or so later, I realized I'd left my Armani jacket in the locker," Abigail said with a sigh. "My husband was going to be in the area on the weekend so I asked him to go and fetch it. What a bad decision that turned out to be," she said viciously.

"Why is that?" Stella asked.

"Paul brought me the jacket on Saturday, and he said he'd seen something very surprising when he picked it up."

"What did he see?"

Abigail glanced toward the lounge door and then lowered her voice. "He said that when he walked in, Trevor had actually been making love to one of his clients, right there on the platform at the back of the cycle studio. My locker is very near the entrance, so they didn't notice him. But he saw them, and was astounded. He said he was glad that I'd quit the class if the instructor got up to this kind of nonsense in public with paying clients."

"Were you worried that he would ask you if Trevor had ever made a move on you?" Stella then asked curiously.

"The answer is yes," Abigail hissed. "Of course I was worried! Like most men, Paul can be jealous and possessive at times. In fact, one of the reasons he liked me doing the spin class was that it was for women only. He could so easily have realized that Trevor was a – a serial cheater. It could have had serious consequences for my marriage. The irresponsibility was simply unreal, and I was furious about it."

"Did Paul see who Trevor was with?" Stella asked, noting Abigail's surge of anger.

"He did. He said Trevor was with Isabella." Raw hatred filled Abigail's voice as she spat out the name. "Paul recognized her instantly. He said he didn't understand how Trevor could be fooling around in public with a married woman who taught kids. He was very surprised by his behavior. I was more than surprised. I was appalled at both of them, particularly her. I told him that we should pull my daughter from the modeling classes."

"And did you?" Stella asked.

Abigail shrugged angrily. "I would have loved to do that. But Paul then said there's nowhere else to go in the area. That class is very convenient and it's the best, and we should just be practical and try to look past this. Ultimately, Paul pays the bills, so in the end we left it as it was."

Abigail sounded as if she was very unhappy about Paul's decision. Perhaps that had been a contributing factor, Stella wondered. She could imagine the emotions that had stormed through her. She would have felt jealousy, inferiority, and a deep fear.

What about the need for revenge? That was now the critical issue.

"Were you angry about Trevor and Isabella?" she asked.

"I was livid. I wished I could have made different decisions, and seen earlier who he really was. And as for Isabella, what a slut! I know I shouldn't speak ill of her but I was, and am, furious!"

It was time to close in on the actions Abigail had taken.

"Where were you yesterday morning?" Stella asked.

"Yesterday morning?" Abigail seemed briefly puzzled by the question.

"That's correct."

"I took my children to school."

"Where do they go?"

"My youngest attends Little People kindergarten on Hayward Avenue, and the two older children are at the private school on Melrose Avenue."

"What time did you take them?"

"I left here about a quarter to eight. The private school starts at eight."

Stella listened carefully. Abigail's travels had taken her to two schools within the area. What had she done after dropping the children off?

"And when did you return home?"

"Straight away. I had to let the housemaid in. She called me to say she'd forgotten her front door key. I got back about eight-fifteen, I think, and after that, I rushed to the local gym and trained there for an hour with a friend. We meet up at eight-thirty on Tuesdays."

"Thank you."

Stella felt crushed by disappointment. Abigail had the motive and the means to have murdered Isabella. But the timeline didn't allow for an unscheduled visit to her home.

There was a chance Abigail could be lying, especially since she lived such a short distance away from Isabella. Stella knew she would have to check with the friend and the housemaid – who could both be covering for her – and also with the gym and the school, who would provide unbiased information.

At a glance, though, her movements were fully accounted for.

"I don't have any further questions. Please give me the contact number for your housemaid and also the name of the gym, and the friend you trained with."

"Of course. You won't mention what we discussed, though?" Abigail asked anxiously.

"No, I won't mention anything."

With the information in her notepad, Stella stood up, feeling as if the weight of the world was pressing down on her shoulders. All three of the women who'd quit the class so suddenly had reasons or alibis.

As Stella walked to her car, her phone rang. Seeing Maxwell on the line, she grabbed it eagerly. With her own leads having disappointed so badly, she hoped he'd had better success.

"I got nowhere. I'm going to check out the third suspect's alibi as soon as I'm in my car, but it's looking strong. Did you have any luck with Trevor's timing?" she asked.

Maxwell sounded disgusted. "Guy's telling the truth," he said in tones resonating with disbelief. "The camera footage at the café shows him arriving at eight-ten a.m. So he did drive straight there. He placed his order at eight-twenty. Two poached eggs and a side of asparagus salad. The waitress remembers him because he always orders custom dishes that are very healthy. His card payment was processed just before nine a.m."

"That's pretty watertight," Stella said. The timing didn't leave any window of opportunity at all.

"He's such a strong suspect. I seriously can't believe he couldn't have done it," Maxwell said. "I thought it would just be a matter of confirming how and when he'd gone to Isabella's house. Now we're back to square one. Let's head back to New Haven, pow-wow with Roth, and try figure out the next step."

CHAPTER TWENTY

When Stella arrived at the FBI New Haven branch, she remembered with a jolt that Carrie would be stationed in the lobby, seething with resentment at being chained to her desk while Stella helped with the investigation.

Worst of all, she hadn't been any help so far. Trevor had a rock solid alibi and so did everyone else with a motive to commit the crime. Even Abigail's alibi had checked out perfectly when she'd called the friend, the school, the housekeeper and the gym. And now, she'd have to run the gamut of Carrie's critical scrutiny.

But, when she headed down the corridor and walked into the lobby to see Carrie working on the files, she was surprised that the tall agent didn't look angry to see her.

She looked up as Stella entered, and stared at her in a thoughtful way.

There was something about her quietly satisfied expression that made Stella's stomach clench.

"Good morning," she said briefly as she passed.

Carrie simply nodded. She didn't say a word, but turned back to her work with a small smile.

That smile made Stella feel seriously worried.

Roth was in the main office, on a phone call which he concluded hurriedly as soon as Stella walked in. Immediately, she sensed the atmosphere, tense and angry.

"Fall," Roth said. "What's going on?" He stared at her accusingly.

Stella stared back in shock. What was happening? She suspected Carrie was causing trouble but she had no idea how.

"I don't understand your question," she said calmly. Inside, she felt sick with panic. What if Carrie had somehow managed to cause serious damage to her fledgling career?

"The state governor called just now," Roth said grimly.

Stella's heart sank. This was Larry Hartford's uncle, a powerful and influential man. She'd hoped that the governor had no connection with Gordon Marshall, who had a personal motive for destroying her career after she'd exposed his own misdoings. But now she feared there was a connection.

Worse still, Gordon Marshall must have presented his version of events to the governor first and of course the governor would believe it, coming from one of his peers in the political world.

So, what had Gordon said? Anticipating a hammer-blow, Stella waited for Roth to tell her.

"The governor was on the phone to me for half an hour. He said that a colleague had given him a very serious warning about corruption in the department, and that he'd heard one of our team was soliciting bribes."

Bribes! Stella couldn't believe it. The corrupt Gordon Marshall was accusing her of the same crimes he was currently defending himself against. What a low, cowardly blow. She felt horrified and ashamed, even though there was no reason for her to feel shame.

It was nothing but mudslinging, but sometimes mud stuck. These accusations, vague as they were, could be incredibly damaging to her reputation.

"The governor was beside himself that this might compromise the current case," Roth continued. "Eventually, I persuaded him to give me the name of the person involved. It was your name." Roth stared at her without a trace of sympathy. His face and voice were as hard as stone.

"Fall, I have no idea how a brand new agent has earned this reputation. I asked him for proof, of course, and he said he would get back to me. But proof aside, tell me now – what the hell is going on and where did this originate?"

Roth sounded furious. He sounded as if his mind was made up, that he believed her to be guilty and that he regretted the day he'd ever asked her to be part of his team.

Fighting her panic, Stella forced herself to remain calm. This was Roth's questioning technique. He was putting her under pressure so that she would be truthful. Now she knew how it felt to be on the wrong side of him at his most forceful.

It felt intimidating. It felt terrifying.

But nobody could fabricate evidence that didn't exist. At any rate, so she hoped. They could only fabricate destructive rumors.

Even so, she couldn't bring Carrie's name into this. Despite the fact she was sure Carrie was involved in spreading the rumors, it would look like Stella was trying to smear a fellow agent. Any negative action would reflect badly on her now. It would be better not to mention Carrie at all, but simply to explain the back story.

"I'm sorry. Until now, I didn't think it was relevant to mention my past," she began.

He pounced on the word with a scowl. "Your past? You have a past that you didn't disclose, despite the background checks and the criminal clearance and the polygraph testing that all new agents undergo?"

"Let me explain, please." Stella took a deep breath. "You might have heard of the Vaughn Marshall murder case, a few months ago?"

"Vaughn Marshall. The ex-senator's son in Greenwich?"

"That's correct."

"The case never made it to the FBI office. As I recall, there was pressure on us to get involved, but it was solved before we did. But how is this relevant?"

She took a deep breath, hoping Roth would accept her version.

"I was Vaughn's fiancée at the time."

"You were?" Roth sounded astonished, as if he would never have pegged Stella as belonging within that society. Well, that made two of them.

"We met when I was at university in Chicago," Stella explained. "It was a spur of the moment proposal. I came back with Vaughn to Greenwich, and I was with him on the night of the murder. I woke up and found his body," she said in a small voice.

In a rush, the memories of her horror and panic flooded back. She vividly recalled the sense of denial she'd experienced, her own mind begging that this must surely be a nightmare or hallucination, because it couldn't be real.

Stella paused a moment, fighting the surge of emotion. She couldn't afford for it to affect her now, when she needed to present her case calmly and logically.

"I was obviously the main suspect," she continued, relieved that her voice sounded level. "I decided to investigate on my own, to clear my name."

"On your own?" Now Roth sounded curious.

"Yes. I did what I could. And luckily I was able to work out who'd killed him."

Roth's eyebrows rose. Stella guessed he was putting two and two together. Now he understood why Clem had said she could be helpful in the recent stabbing of Amanda Logan. Perhaps he also realized why Stella had then chosen to apply to the FBI.

"That sure didn't make the news," he said in a calmer voice.

"I didn't want it to. I was just glad to get out of there and away from them." Stella took a deep breath. "While I was investigating, as a result of what I uncovered, there were some, er, some other irregularities that were exposed regarding the Marshalls."

"Yes, I recall reading that in the news."

"They blamed me for bringing them down." Stella didn't add that they quite rightly blamed her. If it hadn't been for her, the Marshalls would no doubt have continued with their misdoings.

"Okay. I see the background."

"I think they would prefer that I was not part of the state's law enforcement," Stella said tactfully. "Especially not now, while the investigations into them are still ongoing."

"This talk of corruption. Is there any reason for it? Any reason at all, Fall? Telling me is the wisest course of action. This is not the time to hide anything, however minor you might think it to be."

Stella shook her head. "There's no reason at all. I guess it's an easy way to cause reputational damage and sow doubt. It's no coincidence that Gordon Marshall is currently defending himself against corruption charges."

Yet again, Stella felt small and scared when she thought about the might of the Marshall family, and the massive resources of cash and connections that they could muster in their defense. She had nothing at all. And now, she wasn't even sure if Roth really believed her or if these rumors had already planted suspicion in his own mind, and a feeling that there must surely be two sides to this.

Roth nodded. Stella could see he was thinking hard. Was he going to recommend she transfer elsewhere, she wondered suddenly. So soon after starting her career, a transfer wouldn't look good on her work record. Plus, she valued the team and valued Roth. And also, Maxwell. Surprisingly, the thought of never seeing Maxwell again made her feel suddenly lonely.

Of course, the other decision might be to pull her from this case, and from all field work, until the Marshalls' court cases were wrapped up. That could mean years of working in a back office.

Miserably, Stella waited for Roth to reach his verdict, wondering how she could plead her case further.

Clearly, Roth decided he needed time to reach the right decision, because he said, "Thanks for giving me your version. I'm going to do some more research into this myself. As I am sure you can see, this could be problematic, and there are a few different courses of action I'm considering."

Anxiety twanged within her. Roth might well decide her presence here was too risky. He seemed like he was leaning that way. How could she change his mind, when he had his entire department with all its politics to consider? She was just one new girl.

She felt bitterly resentful toward Carrie for her destructive interference. She'd only just started with her smear campaign, and already it was proving wildly successful.

"For now, I'm keeping you on the case," Roth confirmed. "You're part of the team and playing an active role. So we must go forward, and focus on what's important." He sighed. "Solving this crime will be first prize. With a positive outcome, we'll have far more options than if we fail, or this case goes cold."

Stella understood the implications, and felt even more regretful that she had no positive news to report.

"Unfortunately, my theory hasn't come through," she admitted. "I was so convinced the motive had to be jealousy. But all the suspects I interviewed have alibis."

"Yes. It's a good motive. In theory," Roth grimaced, as if he knew only too well how even the best theory could smash to smithereens on the jagged rocks of reality. "It's frustrating. It happens. We've investigated the most logical and obvious avenues. Now we have to sift through the evidence and try again."

Investigation was hard and unforgiving work, Stella thought, heading to one of the desks. The only certainty was that this hadn't been a random crime. Given that Isabella must have been murdered by someone who knew her, she now needed to search for what they had missed.

The clock was ticking. Not only the case, but the future of her career in New Haven, depended on finding the killer.

CHAPTER TWENTY ONE

Opening the case folder, Stella started with the document on top, which was the list of Isabella's calls. Since Isabella had deleted most of the history on her phone, this was important information. The list must have just arrived. Probably, nobody had yet had a chance to review it.

Feeling determined, she decided to approach this with the mindset that there was critical evidence hidden here and she just had to find it. Carefully, she read through the list.

Immediately, the calls and texts to and from Trevor's number jumped out at her. There had been regular calls and messages over the past weeks, and Stella noticed that far more of them had been from Isabella's side. She remembered Trevor had said that Isabella had proved to be high-maintenance trouble, and this definitely confirmed it. She'd been playing a dangerous and reckless game. No wonder she'd been in the habit of deleting her call logs.

Apart from that, she hadn't made or received many calls, and the ones she had made were mostly local. Checking the numbers, Stella saw the most frequent communication was with the arts school. There were beauty and hair appointments, and two private residence numbers in the San Francisco area that repeated again and again on the list. Stella remembered Larry had said Isabella's family lived there.

Was there any detail here she was missing? Stella's gaze drilled into the paper.

What was this one, she wondered.

It was a short incoming call. It had lasted only ten seconds, and Isabella had taken the call on Sunday evening. That had been just two days before her death.

Most probably it was just a wrong number or misdial, Stella thought, given the brevity of the conversation. Almost certainly, there was an innocent reason for this call, from a number that didn't appear anywhere else in the list.

It couldn't hurt to check, she decided, and it would be lazy to assume. Imagine if assuming meant that she missed out on a crucial detail? She wasn't going to let that happen.

She looked up the cellphone number on the database, and the information she needed flashed onto the screen almost immediately.

The number was registered to a man called Charles Hamilton-Cross. Checking the address details and now feeling slightly intrigued, Stella noted that he was a New York resident.

There didn't seem to be any further information on him, other than that he was thirty-two years old and owned a home in Cobble Hill, Brooklyn. She couldn't see what he did for a living.

It might be important to find out who he was. Unfortunately, the first point of contact she'd have to use was the emotional and outspoken Larry Hartford. Who, with his connections, just happened to be the last person she wanted to speak to right now.

Feeling sick with nerves, she picked up the phone and dialed, hoping that after hearing these rumors, Larry wouldn't react badly to the mention of her name.

"Hartford." Larry sounded terse and unhappy.

"Mr. Hartford, it's Stella Fall here from the FBI," Stella said.

She didn't get any further before Larry anxiously interrupted her. "What's happening? Have you found the killer? And what's the deal with this talk of corruption that my uncle called me about just now? I can't believe this is happening. He said it was undermining the case. Is it you? Are you the one involved?" he said, now sounding angry.

Stella felt a rush of dread that Larry's uncle was being so vocal on this point, and that he was accepting the false facts that someone – either Gordon Marshall or perhaps one of his friends – was feeding him. This did not bode well.

"None of the team is involved in anything irregular, myself included. We are all working as hard as we can to solve this crime," Stella said firmly.

"That's not what he said," Larry argued. "He said this was a very serious issue and he was shocked when he heard the allegations."

Stella didn't like the tone of his voice. Larry was emotional and spoiling for a fight. He was looking for a target to vent all the anger and misery he'd endured since his wife's death,

"Agent Roth will be in touch with you later to explain," she said hurriedly, hoping to steer the subject to safer ground. "I'm contacting you for another reason, regarding Isabella's recent call list."

"Go on?" Larry said.

Stella continued as quickly as she could. "On Sunday night, Isabella took a call from a number belonging to a man called Charles Hamilton-

Cross. I'm investigating all her calls, and I wondered if you know who he is?"

There was a short, resounding silence. And then Larry let rip.

"Seriously? That loser called her again?"

"It was a very short call," Stella explained.

"Darn right, it would have been. That criminal, obsessive, immature loser is her ex," Larry shouted. He was venting again, but thankfully not at her.

"Her ex?"

"Her ex-fiancé," Larry said, sounding even more upset now. "What the hell was he doing getting back in touch with her? They haven't spoken since she got a restraining order against him, soon after we were married! He's not allowed to contact her at all! He should be jailed for that."

Stella felt herself go cold.

An obsessive ex fiancé? A restraining order? These were critical details that could have huge significance for the case.

"Can you explain the history to me, please?" she said, quickly grabbing a pen.

"They met when Isabella was still modeling full-time. I don't remember exactly what he did. Trust fund kid, I think, with a few business interests he ran like hobbies," Larry sounded scornful. "They dated for a couple of years. In fact, they were engaged when Izzy and I met. She was unhappy. She wanted out. Out of modeling, out of the engagement. She was dissatisfied with her life. Anyway, we had this, like, instant attraction between us, and after just a couple of weeks, she broke it off with Charles. We were married a month later, and Charles didn't take it well."

"What did he do?"

"He started harassing her. Threatening her. Texts, voicemails," Larry's voice resounded with contempt. "Funny how a guy who claimed to love someone so much could turn so nasty. He called her at all hours of the day and night, screaming that she was a slut and a cheater. He threatened he would destroy her career, that he'd been responsible for two of her big contracts, that she'd never work for any of the top houses again. Which was hilarious, seeing she wanted to quit anyway. And he got destructive, too. He smashed her car window. He staked out the house for hours." Larry gave a short, mirthless laugh.

"What did you do?"

"Izzy packed everything he'd given her into a parcel and shipped it back to him via FedEx. Then I got my lawyers involved, and we got a domestic violence restraining order against him. So as per that order, he was not allowed to communicate with her, or contact her in any way. She then blocked his email and all his numbers."

"How did he respond to that?" Stella asked.

"He disappeared. We never heard from him again. He's been out of our lives ever since then. That was why I didn't think to tell you about this. He was past tense. History."

Until he wasn't, Stella thought, feeling shivers prickle down her back.

"I can't believe he called her again." Larry sounded outraged. "He must have gotten a new number."

"I'll check that out," Stella said.

"Sunday night, you say? I'm sure she'd have told me about it, but I was already on my way to Philadelphia." He paused. "She would have told me when I got back. I'm sure. That was unacceptable. Unacceptable."

He sounded thoughtful, as if he had forgotten Stella was there at all.

"You know, that was the only issue with Izzy," he then said. "She was flypaper for men. She couldn't help it, of course, but they lost her minds over her. Weirdos and obsessives included. And normal guys as well, sometimes. Being married didn't make a difference. I wish I'd known this asshole was chasing her again."

"Thank you so much for this information. I'm going to follow up on it immediately," Stella said.

"Please let me know," Larry sounded concerned now.

She put the phone down with renewed determination flaring inside her.

A highly unstable ex who'd threatened Isabella in the past had called her. Two days later, she'd been murdered.

She needed to track down Charles Hamilton-Cross, urgently.

CHAPTER TWENTY TWO

What steps should she take to locate Isabella's abusive ex, Stella wondered. Roth had rushed out of the office directly after confronting her, and Maxwell hadn't come back yet. Every moment counted now. Should she wait for Roth? Or should she take action and hope she did the right thing?

Agonizing over what to do felt even more pressurized when every wrong decision would be scrutinized by Roth, and would count against her. She couldn't do anything that might cause anyone to think she was corrupt or incompetent.

Miserably, Stella realized that this excessive pressure was not conducive to clear thought at all. She was in a panic.

Forcing herself to calm down, she closed her eyes for a moment and thought logically about the situation. Charles had to be located as a matter of urgency. Therefore, Stella had to start the process. There was no need to confirm this with Roth. The first step should simply be to find out if he was at his home.

Quickly, she turned to the laptop, and looked up the closest police department to his Brooklyn address.

That proved to be the 76th Precinct. With urgency simmering inside her, Stella called them.

"FBI Agent Fall here. Could I please speak to your station commander?" she asked, feeling that it would be best to go straight to the top.

A moment later, she found herself speaking to a deep-voiced, competent sounding man.

"Detective Clint here."

"Agent Fall from New Haven," she said. "We're busy with a murder investigation. We have a person of interest who is a resident in your precinct. I wonder if you could check up whether he's at home?"

"Sure," Detective Clint said.

"His name is Charles Hamilton-Cross, and this is his home address." Stella read it out carefully. "If you find him there, please could your officers escort him to the precinct? We need to question him urgently."

"There's a patrol car in the area now. I'll ask them to head there straight away, and call you back," Detective Clint said.

As Stella put the phone down, Maxwell walked in, closely followed by Roth.

"I've got a meeting with the governor in an hour," Roth said in frustration. "He wants a progress report. This couldn't have happened at a worse time."

"Can't you delay it?" Maxwell asked.

"I can't. Better to get it over with," Roth said, sounding resigned. "We're going to have to release Trevor Urban now. I've just completed the paperwork. With a rock-solid alibi, he's off the list. So that means as of this moment, we have zero suspects in custody and nothing to show to the governor."

"I've got something here, Roth," Stella said, and saw his expression brighten.

"What have you found?" he asked.

"A completely new lead," Stella told them. "Isabella had an ex-fiancé, Charles Hamilton-Cross, with a restraining order against him. Two days before she was killed, he violated the order and called her."

Roth's eyebrows shot up. "How did you find this out?"

"I checked the call list," Stella explained, hoping she'd redeemed herself in his eyes after the attempted character smear. "It was a very short call. Most probably, she would have hung up when she realized who it was. But that could have made him angry. Maybe he decided to retaliate with an in-person visit."

"What action have you taken?" Roth asked.

Stella felt relieved that Roth trusted her to take this matter forward on her own.

"Charles lives in Brooklyn. I've asked the local police department to take a drive to his home. If he's there, they will bring him in."

"Great work," Roth praised her. "Let's hope he's home. If so, we need to get there as fast as we can to question him. We're running out of time on this, and I'm under pressure on all fronts."

He glanced at Stella meaningfully and she felt her stomach twist. The swift release of their only suspect was going to cement the governor's suspicions that something irregular was going on.

Her phone rang, and she grabbed it.

"Stella Fall," she said expectantly.

"It's Detective Clint," her new contact from the Brooklyn said. "My officers have reported that Hamilton-Cross's home is locked up. Nobody is there."

"Thanks for the information. Appreciate you getting back to me so fast," she said, feeling disappointed.

She put the phone down and turned to Roth and Maxwell.

"He's not home. Surely there's a chance he's around here somewhere. Perhaps he called her knowing that he was going to be in this area."

Roth sprang into action.

"Okay. Let's see if we can track him down and confirm his whereabouts. Maxwell, check what vehicles are registered in his name. Fall, it's a small chance, but you can start with calling the major hotels in the area. I'm going to get some visual ID on him so we know who he is and what to look out for, and then see if we can triangulate his phone."

In a moment, the office became a hive of activity. Stella pulled up a map of the major hotels. Her heart briefly sank. There were a few in Branford, and what looked like hundreds in New Haven. She didn't want to think about the amount of time this would take. Time they didn't have. But there was only one way to whittle those numbers down, and that was to start calling.

"Here's what he looks like." Roth pressed a button and Charles's image flickered onto the screen. It was an ID photo. Head and shoulders. The blond man stared unsmilingly at the camera. He had a square face and a strong jaw. A distinctive face, Stella thought. He was a good looking guy, with his regular features and straight nose. She stared at it, impressing his looks into her mind so that she could recognize him at a glance.

"Now for the phone," Roth said, logging into another database. But a moment later, he gave a frustrated sigh.

"Turned off. Or at any rate, not on the network right now," he said.

Stella wondered if that was significant. Had Charles deliberately turned it off so he couldn't be traced?

Feeling even more determined to track him down despite this stumbling block, she returned to the list of hotels she'd compiled. What hotel would be the most likely, she wondered, thinking of how she could speed up this time-consuming process. Charles was a trust fund kid, Larry had said. Therefore, he would be able to afford more expensive hotels and would probably choose them as a matter of course.

All this was dependent on the fact that he'd not preplanned the murder, that it had been a crime of passion. If he'd preplanned, then he would have covered his tracks. But Stella reminded herself that nothing about that scene had looked preplanned.

Would Isabella have let an ex-fiancé who'd threatened her into her home? That was another point to consider, Stella decided, as she dialed the first hotel. Perhaps he'd told her he'd come to say sorry, but when face to face with her, old emotions had flared. That would make sense.

"He owns two cars. A black Range Rover and a silver Porsche," Maxwell said, just before the first five-star hotel answered her call.

"It's Agent Stella Fall here, from the FBI," she said. "I'd like to confirm if you have a certain guest staying with you at this time?"

The receptionist drew in a quick, startled breath.

"From the FBI?" she repeated. "Um, yes, sure. I – I can't give that information out myself. For reasons of privacy. I'll have to refer you to my manager."

"Sure," Stella waited.

"He's meeting with suppliers, and will only be back this afternoon at three p.m.," the receptionist said, sounding regretful.

"Please ask him to call me, urgently." Stella gave the receptionist her number and disconnected, feeling frustrated as she stared at her long list.

Guest privacy was definitely a stumbling block. For the average hotel receptionist, being in trouble with the manager was more of a real and direct threat than being in trouble with the FBI.

Was there a quicker way, she wondered. Perhaps Charles had left some clues on social media. With his distinctive double-barrel last name, it would be easy to search for his profile.

Changing tack, she logged into her own profile, and searched the main sites.

Charles didn't seem to have a profile himself, but as Stella scrolled through the list of names, she noticed that there was a thirty-four-year-old man, Aidan Hamilton-Cross, living in Milford.

"Look what I've found," she called to Maxwell. "Do you think there's a connection here?"

He was at her side in a moment.

"Got to be related," he said. "They look similar. Both big, blonde guys. Could even be brothers?"

Roth hurried to the screen. Peering over their shoulders, he nodded. "You two, look up Aidan's home address and take a drive over there now."

Maxwell turned to the other laptop, his fingers flying over the keyboard as he searched for the home address.

"Ask him if he knows Charles, and if so, whether he's been in touch recently," Roth continued. "Remember, if his brother is the killer, Aidan might know, and might be covering for him. In that case, be tough with him. We don't have time to listen to lies, and we can't afford to spend weeks tracking down a fugitive."

"Got it. Let's go," Maxwell said.

Hoping that their run of bad luck was over now, and that Aidan would lead them to Charles, Stella rushed out behind him.

CHAPTER TWENTY THREE

It was midday by the time Stella and Maxwell arrived at Pinnacle Road, where Aidan Hamilton-Cross lived. Stella's stomach was knotted with nerves. Everything was riding on the next few minutes, including her career future.

She imagined Roth, now in the meeting with the governor, fielding his suspicious questions and trying to convince him that no, the lack of progress was not because the new agent, or any of the team, was taking bribes.

Pinnacle Road was an attractive suburban avenue. The two-story homes had large, well-kept yards, and Stella saw many of them had colorful swings, jungle gyms and see-saws. This was a neighborhood for well-off families. There was a small shopping center at the top of the road, with a park opposite.

"Number twenty is a few houses further on," she said, checking the numbers as Maxwell drove, realizing her mouth felt dry.

"We're going to go in strongly. Whoever's at home, we find out from them where Aidan is and we lean on him hard. We don't play the nice guy," Maxwell said determinedly.

"Agreed," Stella said. Charles's threatening behavior toward Isabella proved that he was not a rational or accommodating person. He wouldn't cooperate quietly with law enforcement. He was likely to pressure his family into lying for him.

His face showed his character, she thought, remembering the photograph and thinking of the hard expression in his eyes.

Her gun was digging into her hip and she shifted position slightly, adjusting the holster. Then she sat straighter as the house came into view.

It was an attractive and well-kept home, with pristine, white-painted boards and symmetrical windows. And outside, parked in the driveway was Charles's Range Rover. Stella felt breathless with shock as she stared at the gleaming, jet-black vehicle.

"It's his car. The same plate," she said quietly, double-checking the number she'd written down.

“Well, will you look at that?” Maxwell said. His voice was deliberately calm but she could sense the tension ratcheting up in his body. Maxwell was on full alert. She felt the same. Her heart was pounding and her hands were cold.

“No Mr. Nice Guy,” Maxwell reminded her as he parked close behind the Range Rover – all the better to prevent a getaway, Stella realized – and climbed out.

They strode up to the house and Maxwell rapped sharply on the front door.

There was silence for a while, apart from the chorus of birds in the trees, and the distant sound of children playing and dogs barking. How weird it was to hear normal sounds at a time of such high tension, Stella thought. Every muscle in her body felt ready for action.

The opening of the door could lead to a deadly confrontation.

A car swished past on the road behind them, making her jump. She strained her ears as she listened for footsteps from inside. Then, with an uneasy sensation that they were being watched, she glanced up.

Was that a shadow at the upstairs window? Stella thought she’d seen brief movement from behind the glass.

She stepped back and looked again.

Impatiently, Maxwell knocked a second time on the door.

Stella was sure that there had been someone looking out from upstairs. And she was becoming more certain that nobody was going to open the door to them. But what did that mean? Was Charles going to hide inside and hope they went away? Or was he seeking out a weapon before he flung the door open?

She had no idea what level of crazy this man was. Hopefully not that much of crazy, but the risk was always there. She could see Maxwell was anticipating it too. His right hand was now resting on the butt of his gun and he was listening intently for any sounds from behind the polished wooden door.

The tension hung heavy in the chilly afternoon air.

Nobody was coming to the door. This was growing obvious. What was happening? Was Charles setting a trap?

She stepped back to see if she could get a better view of upstairs, and it was then that she saw the movement out of the corner of her eye, from the slice of backyard that was visible on the left.

It was nothing more than a glimpse of something being where it shouldn’t. Her puzzled brain took a moment to interpret what her eyes had seen.

It had been a shadow. A flicker of movement. Had it been a dog, she wondered. But there had been no barking.

And then, her mind caught up. That shape had been a man, vaulting the split-pole fence that separated this home's backyard from its neighbors.

"Maxwell! He's a runner!" Stella shouted. "He's just vaulted the back fence!"

Maxwell swore quietly. And then he was off, powering across the grass, sprinting for the fence.

Indecision filled Stella as she ran behind him. What could she do? How could she be most effective? Would climbing the fence be the best option? Should she take the car and drive around, try to catch him on the next street, she wondered, before deciding against it.

Parked behind the Range Rover, Maxwell's unmarked was a strategic barrier that prevented this man from using his vehicle. He must have seen that when he looked out of the upstairs window which was why he'd chosen to run. The unmarked needed to stay where it was.

Therefore, she must join the chase.

Stella had reached the fence. It was high and sheer. She leaped for the top, grabbing it with her palms, feeling the rough layer of dirt that had settled on the well-oiled wood.

There wasn't much in the way of footholds, but her desperately scrabbling feet found a gap in the boards that gave her the purchase to hoist herself up. She was on top, teetering on the edge, with the view of the neighbor's backyard tilting below her as she dropped, feeling the wind rush past her, landing in a crouch on a patch of long, unkempt grass. She gasped for air, breathing the wet, earthy fragrance of the crushed blades and disturbed mud. Then she looked up to see Maxwell hurtling across the grass and heading for the road. He was in pursuit of a tall, blond man wearing a leather jacket and blue jeans.

Brown jacket, blue jeans, blond hair. Stella sprinted furiously across the neighbor's lawn, hearing a surprised cry from inside the home. She wondered if the occupants would call the police. Calling the police would be a good thing, now. They might need help, if Charles got away. They couldn't lose sight of him. If he fled the area now, the investigation might stall for days or weeks.

"Stop! FBI!" Maxwell yelled, but his shouted words only spurred Charles on. He pounded at full tilt down the sidewalk. Maxwell was super-fit and trained, but Charles was a taller man with long legs, which gave him an advantage. And Stella would have to try and keep pace with both of them.

She powered out of the neighbor's front yard, glad to hit the firmer terrain of the sidewalk. Then she sprinted after the two men with all the speed she possessed.

Her legs burned as she flung herself forward. She couldn't outrun Charles over a short distance. But there was nowhere for him to go over a short distance. Right now, he was fleeing in panic. Did he have a plan? Where might he go?

A car passed by, blaring its horn at the running men, and then accelerated away, the driver clearly choosing not to get involved. Stella felt a moment's horror over the thought that Charles might get away, if he had friends who were driving past and who allowed him to jump in. He was just far enough ahead for that to work.

As Stella strained for more speed, she started forcing her breathless brain to work. Think, she told herself. Charles had started running without a plan. He'd been in a panic and looking to flee. But he would soon realize that he needed a plan, or else Maxwell would catch him right there on the street.

They were approaching a crossroad. It was a quiet street. She saw Charles look around, glancing left and right as he stumbled down the curb. Then, decision made, he veered left and pounded down the road with a renewed burst of speed.

He was fleeing toward the shopping center she'd noticed earlier. He must be hoping that he could lose them there, or take a shortcut through the small strip mall.

She slowed to a jog, gasping, her heart pounding in her chest.

If he was formulating a plan, so should she. She shouldn't follow him into the center but should try and anticipate where he would come out. Perhaps she should detour onto the street further down, the one that ran behind the center. That way, his exit route would be blocked.

It was a rogue decision and it ran the risk of failure, but she was not going to catch up with Maxwell so it was the only plan she could think of.

Stella broke into a run again, heading down the back street. Everything was so normal. Two shoppers were heading out with carrier bags in their arms; a school bus eased past on the road. It was a routine afternoon in suburbia, and they were chasing a suspected killer.

Stella rushed past the shoppers. Where would Charles have gone?

"Everything okay, honey?" one of them called, but she didn't sound particularly concerned.

The only place he could use to shortcut through the mall was the arched corridor at the center point. Looking frantically around, she saw there was no other obvious route through and no sign of Charles. Perhaps he'd gone the other way, she wondered, feeling as if she'd made a serious misjudgment by taking a different direction.

Messing up now carried such serious consequences. She'd have to dash into the mall and hope she could see where he and Maxwell had gone.

She rushed in the direction of the center passage, and as she neared it, there he was, running through it toward her.

Her plan had worked, and now she was in front of him. He'd been bracketed.

His face was crimson, gleaming with perspiration, but looked set and furious. Maxwell had gained some ground in the dash through the center, but was still fifty yards behind him.

She rushed toward him.

"Stop! This is an order! Stop!" she screamed.

She really didn't want to draw her weapon. Drawing a gun in a suburban shopping mall would cause so many complications at a time when she was under scrutiny. At this moment, she couldn't risk firing a warning shot and being labeled reckless and irresponsible. Hopefully, she wouldn't need to, because Charles would realize he was now trapped between the two agents.

Charles looked up and saw her. He looked alarmed, but he didn't slow his speed. And he was running fast.

Then, Charles decided to force his way past her.

He charged forward, shoulders pumping, clearly calculating that he was almost double her weight, and was fast enough to avoid her, and if he didn't, he could barge his way past.

It was too late to wish she'd drawn her gun. Now she had only an instant to try and stop him. The only way would be to use her own speed to knock him off his feet.

Gulping a deep breath, she rushed toward him, forcing a last burst from her exhausted legs, determinedly holding the trajectory that would send her cannoning into his left shoulder.

This was going to hurt, Stella thought, as she reached him, ducking under his flailing arm, forcing herself not to slow down.

The impact felt like a car crash. It flung her off her feet and she rolled. Her shoulder slammed into the concrete floor, her elbow crushed against the unforgiving ground, her head bashed against the wall. With pain flaming in every part of her body, Stella scrambled dizzily to her feet again.

She'd managed to knock Charles down. He had stumbled onto his knees, overbalanced, and then sprawled forward onto his outstretched hands. He was swearing furiously, heaving himself to his feet again but at that moment, with ferocious intent, Maxwell cannoned into him from behind.

With a yell, Charles plunged down again, falling heavily onto the paving, and in a moment, Maxwell was on him, with a knee in his back.

Stella sprinted over and grabbed one of Charles's thrashing arms. He was fit, and fighting with the strength of total desperation, but the two of them had him overpowered.

She managed to slip one of the cuffs over his thick wrist, slick with perspiration. A moment later, Maxwell had the other, and he was contained.

Keeping a firm hold of the cuffs, Maxwell scrambled to his feet, half-pulling Charles into a standing position.

Stella was gasping for breath. Her shoulder was on fire, and she felt dizzy with shock and stress and the exertion of the past few minutes. Looking around, she saw a scattering of shoppers had gathered to view the drama. Nobody was trying to get involved, but everyone was watching the scene play out in fascination.

"We're bringing you in," Maxwell told Charles breathlessly.

As he radioed for police backup, Stella hoped that this last-minute pursuit would get the results they so desperately needed.

Running was a clear sign that Charles was guilty. Now, they needed to take it further, and prove that he was Isabella's killer.

CHAPTER TWENTY FOUR

In the small interview room at the Milford police precinct, where they'd taken Charles because it was closest, Stella saw that the burly man looked scared and deflated. The bully boy who'd charged so recklessly at her was gone. Charles's florid face was still flushed from his exertion. His hair was damp with sweat, and rivulets of perspiration trickled down his cheeks. He couldn't wipe them away, because his hands were still cuffed behind him.

The room smelled of fresh sweat. Lowering herself on still-trembling legs into the seat next to Maxwell, Stella thought it also smelled of fear.

"Are you going to free me?" Charles asked querulously. "What can I possibly do to you, here in this little room?"

"The answer to that is no, we're not freeing you," Maxwell told him shortly. "You forfeited your right to be treated like a normal citizen when you stopped behaving like one."

Charles glowered, but lapsed into silence, hunching his shoulders impatiently as if to prove how agonizing these restraints were.

"You know why you're here?" Maxwell asked.

Stella watched Charles carefully. He knew why he was here, there was no doubt about it. His face flushed dark red again.

"This has to do with Isabella. She reported me to you, didn't she?"

"You called her Sunday," she said.

Charles stared at her with angry resignation.

"Yes. Yes, I did. Okay, I admit it. I broke the terms of the restraining order."

He'd done more than that, Stella suspected. But at least he was willing to admit to the first transgression.

"Why did you do that?" she asked.

"I had a new phone number, I was at my brother's house in the area, and I suddenly thought – let me get in touch with her. I admit, I'd had a couple of drinks. I wouldn't have done it sober, but I had this idea that perhaps we could make things right again. You see, I went off the rails when she took up with Hartford. But recently, I've been hearing rumors from friends of friends that she isn't happy with him."

"Tell us more about why you went off the rails?" Stella asked. She felt encouraged that he was speaking freely.

"Look at the timing! She was cheating with him while still engaged to me. Then the next moment she breaks it off and they're engaged! It was just all too crazy. I couldn't handle it and I said things to her that I regretted. I smashed her car window. I turned into that stalker who everyone hates. I showed a side of me I didn't know I had. I'm not proud of what I did. And it gnaws at me, more so because I can't make things right with her because of the damned restraining order. I mean, it has made me feel so angry."

"So you intended to apologize?" Stella asked.

"I had that in mind, yes."

"How did the conversation go?"

"She answered. I said, 'Hey Isabella, it's me, Charles. I'm in town for a few days. Any chance we can meet up?'"

"And then what happened?"

"She just said: 'What the hell happened to your restraining order? You want me to tell the cops you called?' Then she put the phone down on me. I felt – well, I felt mad. But there was nothing I could do. I took the chance. I tried. But then the next thing, I saw you guys outside the house and I realized she did call the cops on me and I could be in a lot of trouble. I know it can even mean jail time if you break those terms."

This story was confusing Stella. Charles had missed out the middle section of it. He'd skipped straight from the phone call, to the arrival of the FBI.

Unless, Stella thought suddenly, he didn't know about the middle part of the story. That awful possibility was occurring to her.

"So you ran because you saw us?"

Charles nodded. "I had this idea that if you didn't find me there, you'd leave it be. After all, I was planning to drive back home tomorrow. I'm only in Connecticut for a few days, because my aunt is visiting from London. And in any case, it was one innocent call, lasting all of ten seconds!" The aggrieved tone was back in his voice again. "Do you guys not have more important things to do with your time? Are there not real crimes taking place?"

This was no clever fakery. He really didn't have a clue what had played out on Tuesday morning, Stella realized, feeling horrified.

"We are investigating a real crime. Where were you yesterday, between seven-thirty and nine a.m., when Isabella Hartford was murdered?" Maxwell asked sternly.

Stella had never seen a question unleash such a horrified reaction.

Charles stared at Maxwell as if he'd seen a ghost.

"What?" he gasped. "What are you saying? You can't be serious!" He sounded incredulous.

Then he paused, waiting, as if expecting a response. When there wasn't one, he continued in a panicked tone. "Is this some kind of trick? Is it a test? It can't be true! This can't have happened!" He was breathing rapidly. He had literally turned white. All the florid color had drained from his face.

"Murdered? It can't be. How – how did it happen?" His voice was clearly trembling.

Stella believed his response was genuine. So far, he hadn't struck her as much of an actor. His emotions were too much on the surface, unchecked and ungoverned.

"You claim you don't know about this?" Maxwell asked sternly.

"Of course I don't know. I don't follow the news much, and I've been out of communication because my damned phone was stolen when we were at a nightclub on Monday night. They're supposed to be delivering a new one today."

Stella exchanged a glance with Maxwell. He looked the way she felt. Frustrated, but with a reluctant acceptance that this response sounded genuine so far.

"Has it – has it been in the media? What happened? Who did it?" Charles sounded agonized.

"It's filtering out to the media," Maxwell said. Then he repeated firmly, "Your movements yesterday morning. Where did you go and what did you do?"

"I walked my nephews to school. They had to be there by eight."

"What school?"

"The local elementary school. It's about a mile from here, on Crescent Road. They're twins, seven years old. Then I went for a short run, and ended up at Sam's Deli after that, where I met Aidan and his wife and our aunt for breakfast. It's in the mall on the corner. They know us there."

He stared from Stella to Maxwell in deep concern. "I guess you think I did it, after seeing that I called her. I guess that means you don't know who did it? It wasn't that rat bag of a husband, was it? I never trusted him, since he stole her from me. I always thought one day, we'd make it up and she'd be back in my life. She can't be gone! She can't!"

Charles was sobbing in frantic breaths.

Showing some sympathy to his plight, Maxwell unfastened the cuffs and handed him a box of Kleenex. Charles blew his nose hard. Then he buried his face in his hands. Stella saw they were shaking.

"This can't be true," he muttered. "Please, tell me this is some sort of story you're fabricating to test me? Surely it can't be real?"

Stella knew the next step would be to check all possible facets of Charles's account. They couldn't take his word for it and would have to get past the possibility that his family might be covering for him. But even with this legwork still ahead, Stella didn't think he was the killer. He hadn't known about it. He most certainly had not faked his utter shock at the news. Every moment of his appalled reaction had rung true to her.

Plus, given how Isabella had responded to his phone call, it would be very unlikely that she'd have let him into the house. More likely, she would have called the cops straight away if he'd arrived at her home.

Logistically, it didn't add up.

He was the perfect suspect. If only they could arrest him on suspicion of the crime, Stella thought sadly. But they couldn't, and would have to keep looking further.

Despite the overwhelming evidence that had set them on his trail, Charles Hamilton-Cross wasn't the killer. They were not just back to square one now. It was more like square minus one. Especially since Roth had told the governor they were following a promising lead, and raised his expectations.

All other avenues had fizzled out. This case was devoid of workable leads. And, worst of all, time was running out. People would be starting to doubt the capability of the investigation team. And that meant, at a high level, people would be looking for a scapegoat.

Suspicion would be focused on her after this debacle. Rumors were ugly things. All it took was one toxic lie to create a groundswell of antagonism and doubt that could end up overwhelming her.

She'd have to go back to square minus one and start again, but now she felt she was working from a place of total desperation.

CHAPTER TWENTY FIVE

Stella trailed dispiritedly out of the Milford police precinct. The afternoon was breezy and cool. Near the road, a caretaker was sweeping up the last of the fall leaves from the gracious yellow birch trees that lined the sidewalk. Drizzle spattered her face. The cloudy sky was as gray and bleak as her mood.

In her purse, her phone started ringing.

Taking it out, she saw it was Clem on the line. Normally, she would have been pleased to see her mentor calling, but right now, all she could think was that she'd have to admit her failure to him.

On the other hand, Stella thought, you only failed when you stopped trying. Clem himself had reminded her of that at low points in her life, when she'd been grappling with issues in her Master's thesis and the future had felt tenuous and dark.

Plus, Stella told herself sternly, not all criminal investigations could be solved in a day. So she'd damned well better develop the strength of character she needed to see these cases through for the long haul.

"Hey Clem," she said, irritated that she sounded discouraged, despite her best efforts to speak in an upbeat tone.

As usual, he didn't waste time on formalities. "I hear the suspect from yesterday has been released, due to lack of evidence. I wanted to call you to say well done for being right. Your instincts on that were correct."

Stella sighed. At the moment, Clem seemed to have more faith in her instincts than she herself did.

"He was released, but the problem is we now have a total, frustrating lack of anyone else who could have committed this crime," she said. "I had three people in mind. They all checked out, with alibis. Then we came across a fourth suspect in Isabella's call records; an ex with a restraining order against him. And he's just checked out, too."

Even though she tried not to let her voice show her despair, she guessed Clem could hear it.

There was a thoughtful pause.

"You were on the right track originally," Clem said. "Your thinking was logical. Your reasoning was very sound. I personally believe you pinpointed the most likely direction, and motive, for the crime."

"But they all checked –" Stella began, but Clem wasn't done.

"Your first few, most obvious suspects checked out. So then you did a sensible thing based on the new information in your possession. You pursued a different avenue and went after an individual who was a wild card, and who didn't fit in with your original line of thinking. This individual had a history with the victim and a potentially strong motive and so it was reasonable and correct to do that."

Stella thought about his words as she climbed into her car, glad to be out of the chill of the breeze. It was comforting that Clem thought she'd done nothing wrong so far.

"Then that didn't work out," he continued. "Would have been nice if it did. But all it means is that you now need to return to your original thought processes. Because you haven't ruled out everyone. You can't have done. If you continue with that line of thinking, eventually, you will find the right suspect."

Stella acknowledged that Clem was correct. She needed to go back to the beginning and follow her trail of logic all over again.

If jealousy was a motive, Stella reminded herself there were two people who had been involved in the affair. There was Isabella and there was Trevor.

Just as someone from Isabella's past could have caught up with her, so someone from Trevor's past could have done the same.

She remembered her suspicions about Trevor's carefully, cleverly constructed façade. Last time she'd spoken to Clem, he'd mentioned that people build fortifications for a reason. It was time to find out who Trevor Urban really was, where he came from, and what history he had.

*

Pulling up outside the luxury home on Sunset Drive twenty minutes later, she felt a weird sense of déjà vu. She hoped she would find Trevor there alone. At least there were no other cars parked outside this time, which was hopefully a good sign.

When she tapped on the front door, and heard a suspicious voice saying, "Who is it?" Stella guessed he was alone.

"It's Agent Fall from the FBI."

There was a pause, and then the door opened.

Trevor looked far from pleased to see her.

"What do you want?" he asked in a reserved tone.

"I want to ask you a few more questions relating to the case."

Stella was sensing that she was walking into trouble as she entered the home. Something didn't feel right in here, but she wasn't sure what it was.

"You're harassing me again. Why?"

As soon as she'd stepped inside, he locked the front door – a departure from the last time when they'd walked straight into the unlocked home, and turned to face her.

Now, Stella realized he was furiously angry. She could feel it emanating from him, so forcefully that for a moment she feared that he did, in fact, have a violent streak.

"What the hell do you really want, Agent Fall?" he said.

"I told you. I'm researching the case," she said, as calmly as she could.

She felt trapped, with him standing between her and the door. He was cutting off her means of escape, and she thought it was fully intentional, not a subconscious gesture at all.

"Why? What could I possibly tell you that I haven't already? You are interfering in my life. Are you trying to destroy me? Do you know how much damage you've already done? Do you have some kind of a vendetta against me just because of the person I am? Is this a moral crusade for you now? I think it is!" He stepped toward her and it took all Stella's self-control not to step back. She couldn't show weakness now, even though she was terrified. Weakness would be dangerous.

She felt as if she'd accidentally triggered something, but what?

"Who are you really, Trevor Urban?" she asked him, as strongly as she could.

The question jolted him. Surprise, in fact, shock, crossed his face.

Seeing he was between her and the door, there was no point in contesting that space. Instead, Stella turned and walked into the lounge. She was shaking inwardly, but forced herself to appear calm. She chose a seat and sat, clenching her cold hands into fists.

After a short, loaded pause, Trevor followed her into the lounge. He didn't sit. He stood opposite her with his back to the enormous window.

"You don't care who I am. Why would you care? You're an evil, interfering woman who is now hell bent on destroying me because you have issues with my behavior."

Stella felt lacerated by the words, even though she knew he was not directing them at her personally, but at who he thought she represented. Not the law enforcement side, the moralizing side. Trevor was projecting his own insecurities onto her.

Even though she understood why he was doing it, the sharp, scathing criticism made her feel the way she'd done all those times when her mother had verbally laid into her, seeking to crush her, with nothing in mind but to take Stella to a place where she couldn't fight any more.

She didn't think Trevor was seeking the same dominance. It felt more as if he was ultra-defensive, as if he was guarding his own insecurities, deep inside. Once again, she was up against those barricades he'd built.

A hardcore approach would only encourage him to reinforce those walls. She needed to use a softer approach and ask him nicely.

"Mr. Urban, I came here to ask you this favor because I genuinely need your help," she explained calmly.

Stella deliberately used the magical word 'because', knowing that it was effective in persuading people to comply.

In her psychology studies, Stella had been fascinated to learn how much that word could make a difference. A famous Harvard study done decades ago, had shown how people waiting in a line to use a photocopier would allow someone to go ahead of them only 60 percent of the time if they simply asked. But if the person used the word "because," and gave a reason, they were allowed to push ahead over 90 percent of the time. And strangely enough, it didn't even matter how good the reason was. It was simply using the word that had the persuasive effect.

She continued in a steady voice. "To catch the killer, I need as much background information as I can get. An unsolved murder is going to cause ongoing damage to everyone involved. You and me both. All of us."

Trevor stared at her thoughtfully. His anger was ebbing. She didn't think it was an integral part of his character. He wasn't comfortable with being angry. Now that his storm of temper had blown over, he was returning to his normal mindset.

"What sort of background information?" He still sounded suspicious.

"I'm guessing that you are from somewhere other than here? That you moved here recently, probably a few years ago, to open your business?"

Now suspicion changed to surprise.

"Yes. That's right. Four years ago."

"Where did you start out?" she asked.

"I started out working for a gym. I built a clientele very quickly and moved into freelancing. Then I noticed the studio up for sale. It was an old nightclub. I saw the opportunity and set it up."

Stella was impressed. She didn't think Trevor could have impressed her, given that she found his behavior with clients to be despicable, but in terms of business sense, he'd shown both courage, and a talent for identifying and filling a niche in the market.

"Where did you live before this? Were you in a similar line of work?"

Trevor hesitated. Then, to her utter astonishment, he gave an embarrassed laugh.

"Now that's a subject I don't like talking about," he said. "I know you probably think I should be ashamed of my present circumstances. But I'm ashamed of my past."

"Why?" Stella asked.

"I grew up in a real unhealthy family in Atlanta. Your typical TV, soda, fast food consumers. No exercise. No idea of eating well. I was severely overweight as a teen. I was teased terribly at school. I hated myself, but I was stuck in a cycle I couldn't break out of. I only had my first girlfriend when I was twenty-one. She was also very overweight. We basically enabled each other, and when I was twenty-four, I was the heaviest I'd ever been. I tried all the diets. I couldn't stick to anything. Nothing worked. I was insanely depressed."

Stella couldn't believe it. She simply couldn't take in that this charming, muscular, super-fit man had come from such a background. No wonder he hid behind his veneer, she thought, with a surprising flash of sympathy.

"How did you break the cycle?" she asked.

Trevor shrugged. "Trial and error and reaching rock bottom. I finally found the right combination of food and exercise that I could stick to. I read and researched so much on the topic along the way. I started to lose weight and when I saw progress, it encouraged me. I set myself monthly goals. I crushed those goals. Then I set myself fitness and exercise goals, too. A year later, I'd lost all the excess weight. I looked good. I felt great, and I decided to qualify as a fitness instructor."

"Did you move because of a job opportunity?" Stella asked.

Trevor shook his head. "I wanted a clean break. I wanted to start in a place where nobody knew who I had been. I was ashamed of the person I had been and I wanted to forget it. I split up from my girlfriend – Nicole didn't take that well, but I wasn't the same person anymore. We had nothing in common. I was focused on my exercise routines, my new line of studying. She was still stuck in the same place, where she had always been."

"So you got the job here?"

"Yes, that's right. I thought it would be a good move. It was a wealthy area. The salary was above average, and I thought tips would be good. It was only once I got here I started realizing that some of the female clients were – well, lonely. Looking for more than just a personal trainer. And there seemed to be something about me that they liked. I mean, more than that I was a fit guy. I think it was my presence. I always aim to be reassuring as I know deep down what it's like to struggle to change. And of course, I could give lots of help on weight loss." He shrugged. "The opportunities followed and I'll be honest, I didn't turn them down."

"I understand. And are you still in touch with Nicole?" Stella asked.

Trevor smiled ruefully. "She's never forgotten me, and reaches out every couple of weeks. I don't take her calls or answer her messages. Sometimes she updates me that she's well, or forwards fitness news. Sometimes she just sends memes. But other times she gets angry and starts accusing me all over again of treating her badly and demands that we meet face to face. So I prefer not to get into a conversation with her as I'm never sure which way it will go," he said, sounding apologetic.

"I appreciate what you've told me. It's been very helpful," Stella said gently. She had never thought she'd feel any empathy for Trevor, but she was surprised to find that she could – sort of – sympathize with why he had behaved the way he did. He was catching up with the wild teenage and young adult years he'd missed, at what she guessed must be the age of twenty-nine or thirty.

Over and above the interesting tale of personal transformation, the story told her something else as well. It told her that Trevor had someone important to him in his past, who'd been dumped and then ignored.

But Nicole hadn't been ignoring him, and she had been angry.

Stella needed to track down Trevor's ex-girlfriend, immediately.

CHAPTER TWENTY SIX

Stella called Nicole as soon as she was in her car, hoping that the cell number Trevor had given her was still active, because he'd said he hadn't been in touch with her since the break-up.

She cobbled together her strategy in haste, while she was dialing the number. The top priority was to ascertain whether Nicole was in the area, or had been yesterday. It was a very long drive from Atlanta to Branford. Probably over fifteen hours, Stella estimated. Nicole could have driven or flown. If she'd driven, she might not even be home yet.

Either way, Stella needed to confirm her current whereabouts, and then find proof she had embarked on the trip. Perhaps an easy way would be to find out where Nicole worked. If she had a nine-to-five, she would have taken time off. That would be a red flag.

She felt a rush of relief when the call was answered after two rings.

"Nicole Peters speaking?" There was a question in the words. Nicole was sweet-voiced and sounded friendly.

"Ms. Peters, it's Special Agent Stella Fall here from the FBI."

"From the FBI?" Nicole's voice was filled with wonderment, and a note of trepidation.

"That's correct."

"And you want to speak to me?"

First things first, Stella thought.

"What is your current location, please?" she asked, realizing that she could confirm this by calling into the office and seeing if they could triangulate the phone.

She waited in eager anticipation to see what Nicole would say.

"I'm at home," she said, sounding confused.

"Where do you currently reside?"

"I live in North Bridgeport. I'm in a garden cottage, at number five Petunia Way."

"North Bridgeport, Connecticut?" Stella asked carefully, feeling a sense of disbelief.

"That's correct."

Well, Stella thought. Talk about expecting the unexpected. Trevor clearly hadn't known about this and Stella herself was now wondering darkly why Nicole would have made such a move, so close to where her ex lived.

"I'd like to interview you in person please. I have some background questions to ask you."

"Sure," Nicole said. There was a nervous note in her voice now that had all Stella's instincts on high alert.

Stella disconnected, and programmed the address into her GPS. It wouldn't take her long to get there at all.

As she started driving, she called Maxwell.

"Trevor has an ex-girlfriend who he broke up with, and left on bad terms," she explained. "She's moved to a cottage at number five Petunia Way, North Bridgeport. I'm on my way to speak to her now. Do you want to join me?"

"I'll head there right away," Maxwell said, sounding determined.

*

As Stella drove into North Bridgeport, she thought carefully about the best approach to use with Nicole. It would be better for her to come across as gentle and non-threatening, she decided. That way, when Maxwell arrived, he could provide a more forceful and bullying alternative if it was needed.

She parked outside the home, which was an established property that carried a faint air of neglect about it. Either the owners were elderly, or didn't care much for gardening and home improvements, Stella thought, staring at the overgrown grass, scattered with fall leaves. In the distance, the walls of the main house were covered in climbing creepers.

There was a separate wooden side gate marked "Garden Cottage." Opening it, Stella headed up the path, stepping over mossy paving stones with grass overgrowing around them. The sound of birds was like a background shimmer in the cool, damp air.

Stella tapped on the door, realizing that the inevitable mention of Trevor would be a sensitive topic. The break-up must have been devastating to Nicole and although it was years ago, old wounds sometimes didn't heal well.

The door opened, and she stared in shock at the woman who faced her.

"Good afternoon. You must be Agent Fall?" Nicole said.

It was the same person. The same sweet voice. But she didn't look anything like Stella had expected. She'd assumed she would be meeting an overweight woman just as Trevor had described. But Nicole was no longer overweight. Looking at the tanned, fit, slim brunette who smiled tentatively back at her, Stella couldn't believe she ever had been overweight.

Trevor was not the only one who had reinvented himself. She had, too.

"Good afternoon," she said. "Are you Nicole Peters?"

She nodded. "I am, yes."

"Thank you for agreeing to the interview. I'm looking for background information on Trevor Urban. It's in connection with a recent crime." She decided not to use the word 'murder,' but to wait and see if Nicole might choose to use it.

Nicole's eyes widened. Stella could see how her demeanor changed. She suddenly looked guarded. Having faced Stella directly when the door was opened, she now turned away, staring at the tiled floor.

"A crime? Is Trevor under suspicion?" she mumbled.

"Trevor is not a suspect," Stella reassured her.

She noticed that Nicole didn't seem particularly comforted by the news.

"I must say, I haven't heard about – whatever it is. But I'm very busy at work," Nicole added, speaking more rapidly.

She didn't seem to be busy now. It was early afternoon on a Wednesday, and here she was, at home.

"What work do you do?" Stella asked, following her into the cottage. It was a larger and more luxurious place than she'd expected from its modest garden setting. The rooms were spacious. Nicole led the way into a lounge furnished with smart leather couches. Half of the large room did duty as a home gym, with equipment set up on the shiny tiled floor. Stella noticed a spin bike in a place of pride.

Beyond, through an archway, she saw a gleaming stove and a double door refrigerator in the kitchen, even though it seemed like Nicole surely didn't prioritize food any longer.

"I got a new job a few months back. I work as an assistant for one of New Haven's biggest architectural firms."

She smiled, the expression lighting up her already attractive features. "Please, sit."

She didn't sit, but paced energetically to and fro. Perhaps she was anxious, Stella thought.

A new image, a new job. It seemed like Nicole's life was moving in a good direction. She was less sure about why she wasn't at work, in her normal sounding nine-to-five job.

"Are you taking today off?" she asked.

Nicole hesitated. "Yes. I'm due back tomorrow. I took three days of leave to attend to a few personal matters," she said shortly.

"Have you been away at all?"

"No. I've mostly stayed home."

She was pacing faster now. There was something odd about it. Her activity looked borderline frenetic, Stella thought.

Staying home, presumably alone, pointed to the lack of an alibi, but Nicole seemed defensive about this line of questioning, so Stella decided to come back to it at a later stage.

"Why did you choose this area to live?" she asked, hoping to get Nicole to settle, as she seemed to be increasingly wound up.

She did, in fact, stop her pacing while answering the question. In fact, Stella thought she'd realized what she was doing and was now making an effort to stop. She perched on one of the chairs, but her feet shifted and her fingers twined together ceaselessly as she spoke.

"I wanted to be close to the coast. It's been a life goal of mine. Now, I'm a five minute drive away, or a fifteen minute run," she smiled. "And with the big firms, salaries tend to be higher. That's also important to me. I wanted to earn better."

"Did you know that Trevor lived nearby?"

Nicole nodded. "I did know he had moved to this area. But it's a big area and why should I let one ex-boyfriend get in the way of my own dreams?" She spread her hands smilingly. "At any rate, that's what I told myself."

It sounded plausible enough, Stella thought. But she didn't buy it. Nicole's version sounded rehearsed.

"When did you and Trevor split up?" she asked.

Nicole made a rueful face. "It wasn't a mutual split-up. He dumped me and treated me very badly. He literally walked out on me, and it was at a time when my mother was sick – she'd just been diagnosed with diabetes – and I was at a low point in my life. But it was years ago. Maybe four years?"

Stella nodded. This confirmed the timeline Trevor had told her.

"How did you feel at the time?"

"I was devastated, of course. We'd been each other's support ever since we were twenty-one years old. I'd helped him in his weight loss journey. But in a way I think what he did had a positive outcome. It made me decide that if he could change his life, I could, too."

"So you followed the same regime he'd done?" Stella asked.

Nicole nodded, her features tautening into determination. "It was one of the hardest things I'd ever done. I didn't think I could. In a way, I guess I'd idolized Trevor as some kind of Superman." She laughed. "Someone who had the ability to break free from who he had been and become completely different. No way did I believe I had that in me."

Her words interested Stella. By her own admission, the bust-up had been a catastrophe for Nicole. Trevor had hurt her deeply. His rejection had been the trigger that she'd used to completely reinvent her own life. And then she'd moved to the same area.

Even if it had been subconscious, Stella thought she'd chosen that area because it was where he was. But she doubted it was subconscious. This had to have been a deliberate decision.

"How long did it take you to get fit and lose the weight?" she asked.

"It took me three full years. It was such a battle. I had setbacks along the way. In the second year I gained nearly forty pounds and thought it was all over. But then I got back on track again. It's a daily fight. I was addicted to unhealthy eating. I used food in all the wrong ways and had to teach myself the good habits. Diet, exercise, movement."

Stella glanced again at the exercise bike.

"Are you dating anyone at the moment?" she asked.

Nicole shook her head vigorously. "I've been so busy since the move. And I'd rather not date within my work environment. I don't want to complicate my job, if you see what I mean?"

Stella nodded. "Yes, I do understand."

"But anyway, you obviously want to know what I know about Trevor. And I don't think he's a bad person. Look, he treated me appallingly but over time I started to realize that he had his own insecurities to deal with, just as I did."

She half-stood, and then sat back down again, crossing her legs and swinging the left one back and forth, back and forth.

"That's helpful information," Stella said. Even though background on Trevor was not, in fact, the main reason for her visit, she decided to continue with this line of conversation, as it seemed Nicole was opening up and talking more freely. In fact, she seemed eager to talk about him.

It was just her frenetic body language that was making Stella feel creeped out. It was like she was observing two different people at war, she thought. One was trying to keep control and the other kept fighting to break loose. She wondered suddenly if Nicole took stimulant drugs to help with weight loss.

"Was he ever violent or abusive? Did he have a side like that at all?"

"Oh, no. Absolutely not. He wasn't a violent person in the least. He was very gentle. I always knew Trevor was highly intelligent. Even when we were both without a job and we had no money, it didn't stop him from dreaming. He had such great ideas! I never doubted that he would be very successful one day."

Stella looked around the room and it was then that she noticed the photo on the shelf above the fireplace. It was a framed picture of two people whose faces she knew, but who were unrecognizable compared to who they had become.

A younger, very chubby and round-faced Trevor and Nicole, hugging each other tightly.

Nicole had seen the direction of her gaze, Stella saw as she turned back to her, and for a moment she saw a flash of panic in the other woman's eyes.

"He really means nothing to me," Nicole emphasized laughingly. "I keep that photo there because it's one of the very few I have of myself. I was very camera-shy when I was overweight, but that photo reminds me who I was, and who I could be again if I don't watch myself. It's one of my mental techniques for keeping on the right path."

She jumped to her feet, that strange energy surging again. She stared around as if hoping to find an outlet for it. Her gaze rested on the photo frame and she immediately looked away from it, as if she didn't want Stella to look there again either. Whirling away, she headed to the opposite corner of the room where she made a miniscule adjustment to the window blinds.

While she fidgeted unnecessarily with them, Stella found her gaze returning yet again to the spin bike.

Finally, she realized why she was noticing it. It looked to be the exact same model that Trevor had installed in his studio.

The exact same model, all the way down to the silver-chrome seat.

With a rush of conviction, she decided that she didn't believe Nicole's account. She wasn't just withholding information, but telling downright lies.

"You still love him, don't you?" she asked. And then staring at her more sternly, she asked the question again. "I can see you do. The photo. This bike. The fact you moved to this area. Answer me truthfully, please, Nicole, because I will not accept any evasions. I already know you have messaged Trevor regularly since the break-up. What I want to know is whether you took this further. Have you visited him recently? Driven past his place? Whether he was aware of it or not?"

Nicole stared at her mutinously and then turned back to adjust the blind again. The silence stretched out between them. Stella let it ride. Waited for her to start feeling so uncomfortable that she would have to break it.

She'd do so either with the truth or a lie. She had the choice. But she'd already been warned that Stella was watching for the lie.

Stella had no idea what to expect, but she'd never imagined the reaction her words would trigger. Never had she realized how much of an emotional tightrope Nicole had been teetering on.

She whirled back toward Stella, enraged. It was as if she'd had an instant hit of some crazy, mind-altering, stimulant. Her entire body tensed. Her hands raised. Her eyes narrowed. Her mouth curled back and her feet planted themselves on the floor as if she was expecting Stella to attack her.

Stella barely had time to draw a horrified breath at the oncoming avalanche, before the words began spilling out of Nicole's grimacing mouth.

CHAPTER TWENTY SEVEN

"Yes, yes, yes!" Nicole's shouted confession battered Stella's eardrums. "You have no idea what I've been through in the past year. The past years! How he broke my heart, the one man I've always loved. How I scraped myself back together and got the strength to change. You have no idea what that took. It took all of me! I broke me and I remade me and I did it all for him. For that waste of skin, that trash bag, that idiot who made me feel like the most important person in the world, the most needed person, before he dumped me!"

Her voice rose to a scream.

Stella felt the surge of adrenaline she'd dreaded. Nicole's outburst was triggering her own deeply buried memories. She felt haunted by the flashbacks that her mother's treatment had etched into her mind.

Digging her fingers into the couch, she tried to control the sense of panic she felt at witnessing this. Nicole seemed to have forgotten she was there. She'd retreated into a headspace that only she could see.

"So yes! I never stopped messaging him, hoping he'd respond. And yes, I went to see him recently," Nicole screamed. "I wanted to show him who I had become. That I had now earned his love again. Earned it! What an idiot I was."

She was gasping for breath, tugging the blinds back to reveal the calm garden beyond, where a light rain had started falling in the darkening afternoon.

"How stupid was I? How obsessed? How completely fooled I was by him. So yes, it took me ages to gather my courage. Ages. Then I went to him."

"When did you go?" Stella asked. She didn't even know if her question would penetrate, but it did. Nicole swung round and gave her a strangely blank gaze.

"A week ago. I know, so recent. But it took me so long to gather the nerve. I planned it. I dreamed it. I visualized what would happen and how things would play out between us. I'd already driven past his house, of course. I knew where he lived. I imagined us both together, living in that beautiful place, looking out every morning at the sea."

She was gabbling the words out, gasping for breath. Stella was feeling not only terrified, but seriously concerned. She thought Nicole might be experiencing – if not an actual psychotic episode, then something close to it.

But she was committed now. Nicole was wrapped in the past, reliving her story. No matter how rocky this ride proved to be, Stella had no option but to ride along with her, because she wasn't going to stop.

"So you went there? What time?" She hoped that the reference to time might somehow ground Nicole. But it didn't. She didn't even notice the question. She'd retreated too far into her own mind.

"I had it all planned. I knew how it was going to go. I tried so hard. My hair!" She tugged distractedly at her wavy, brunette locks. "My outfit. I wore what he liked. Why did I do it? Why? I got there and I saw a BMW parked outside. There hadn't been one there the first time, so I wondered if he had company. I started freaking out. I was too scared to continue. I was too afraid to ring that bell. I thought I'd check through the window first, see if he was there. And he was. He was sitting on the couch, with this woman. What a slut! He had his tongue down her throat, he was groping her, I knew this must be his new girlfriend. She was beautiful. So beautiful!"

Nicole sounded broken.

Even as she was following this gabbled account, she was agonizing what to do if Nicole's manic behavior got any worse. She would have to try and calm her down and if that didn't work, subdue her. She hoped Maxwell was nearly here.

"Did you knock? Did you speak to him?" Stella asked loudly.

This time, her words managed to get a foothold in Nicole's traumatized psyche.

"No! Why would I do that? He'd dumped me once. Humiliated me once. I decided I didn't need another round of that. But I looked in the car." Now Nicole's eyes narrowed. "I wanted to find out who this woman was, who had stolen him from me. And I found out because I saw leaflets all over the front seat. Her photo was all over them, I recognized her hair. The leaflets advertised modeling courses for kids at the arts school. She ran them. Her name was Isabella Hartford. So, now I knew who she was. And I wanted her dead!"

Stella bit her lip as Nicole's voice rose to a scream.

"I wanted her dead! Dead! I wanted to wrap my hands around her neck and squeeze all the life out of her! How dare she! How dare she shatter my dreams that way!"

Fear began boiling over in Stella. This woman was undoubtedly murderous, but she was not okay. She was semi-delusional and tipping rapidly into insanity. She wasn't even seeing Stella.

Now, Nicole was staring unblinkingly at the photo.

"It was you and me, Trev. You and me. And then, suddenly, it wasn't anymore. Why, why did you betray me that way? With her? Isabella Hartford? An ex-model?"

With astonishing suddenness, Nicole grabbed the photo and flung it to the ground. The glass smashed on the floor.

"It's okay." Stella jumped up. This was enough. She couldn't listen anymore. Her heart was racing. Her own panic threatened to overwhelm her at having to endure this.

Just like the frame, Nicole's fragile grasp on normality had shattered. She'd been obsessed with Trevor. Isabella's presence had pushed her over the edge.

"Just stay calm," Stella tried to grab her arm but Nicole wrenched away from her.

"Don't touch me! Don't touch me! I don't want anyone touching me now!"

Her hand lashed out. Stella wasn't quick enough. She jumped back but Nicole's fingers caught her a glancing blow on her jaw. Her teeth snapped together and she tasted blood in her mouth, realizing she'd bitten her tongue.

"Just stay calm," she pleaded again.

She was going to have to singlehandedly control this madwoman, as she had no idea where Maxwell was.

There were handcuffs on her belt. Stella grabbed them off the loop. Now was the difficult part. She was going to have to get them onto a woman who was beyond reason and tipping over into violence.

Nicole was screaming aloud. "I loved him! Loved him! How did this happen? I wanted the bitch dead! She had to die!"

"We need to bring you into the police station for questioning," Stella shouted. "This is an order. A direct order from an FBI agent. Failure to obey will have serious consequences. Please cooperate, ma'am."

At that moment, to her extreme relief, Maxwell burst into the cottage.

Upon seeing him, Nicole screamed at the top of her lungs – a shrill, terrified, primal sound, and turned to Stella, in full attack mode. Stella ducked out of the way of her flailing arms. Nicole hit her another glancing blow on the head, but Stella was faster this time. She dived sideways, and barely felt it land.

"You are under arrest, ma'am." Maxwell grabbed Nicole's arm. She was shrieking and struggling with the strength of desperation, and it took the two of them to cuff her and manhandle her down onto one of the lounge chairs.

There, at last, Nicole's manic rage seemed to ebb. Gasping great sobs of breath, she stared down at her hands in puzzlement, as if wondering how those cuffs had gotten there.

Quickly, Maxwell radioed for backup.

"You okay?" Maxwell asked.

"I'm fine," Stella said breathlessly.

"I heard her screaming as I arrived. Shouting out that she wanted Isabella to die. I've never heard anything like that," Maxwell sounded shaken. "The fury in her words was off the scale. Were you okay there? Have you experienced that before?"

"Not so suddenly. I think I'm okay, though," Stella said. Her hands were trembling violently.

She felt nauseous, and beyond shocked at what had just played out. She'd never thought, when arriving at Nicole's quaint garden cottage, that she would witness a full-scale psychotic breakdown.

Never before had she heard someone screaming out their intent to murder with so much pure hatred resonating from the words.

That shrieked confession had proven her guilt. She was obsessed with Trevor. She knew who Isabella was and had researched her. She was highly unstable and could have experienced a psychotic episode when confronting Isabella, similar to the one she'd just been through now.

The right suspect was safely in police custody, unable to do harm to herself or to anyone else. The case was concluded, wrapped up in the neatest possible way.

All they had to do was get the details of the murder, seeing Nicole had already confessed in full to the intent.

After all the twists and turns so far, Stella hoped this would be a simple job, and there would be no further surprises waiting.

CHAPTER TWENTY EIGHT

"Excellent work, Fall," Roth praised Stella as soon as he walked into the office where she had already arrived. Nicole Peters had been brought straight to the New Haven FBI office, so they could question her in one of the interview rooms on site. Maxwell was there now, setting things up.

"I'm so glad we investigated her," Stella said.

She had just finished typing out a detailed affidavit, describing the events that had played out at the cottage. It hadn't been easy reliving those moments. Typing the report had taken longer than it should because of her unsteady, trembling hands.

She was utterly shaken by the craziness she'd experienced. Being that close to that level of insanity, having those furious words screamed directly at her, had struck deep chords of fear inside her, triggering memories that made her feel small, helpless and useless all over again. She hadn't realized until this confrontation, how scarred she was from the vicious abuse that her mother had inflicted.

She wanted to be alone, somewhere dark, and burst into tears, curling into a ball and crying until exhaustion and sleep overtook her. Instead, she had to present a professional front to Roth, despite her jittery state and her hands that would not stop shaking.

"You were convinced all along that jealousy was the motive for this crime, and so it's proved to be," Roth said, as he finished checking his folder.

"I thought it had to be, given the person Isabella was," Stella agreed, clasping her hands together firmly.

"We've got more than enough evidence against Nicole Peters already."

"Do we?" Stella said, feeling encouraged that the traumatic experience had at least gotten the results they needed.

"We have the admission of intent to murder, the attempted attack on you, no clear alibi for the time of the killing, and the time booked off work on the day of the crime as well as the days before and after. Also, significantly, I've just had a look through her phone and listed the calls she made."

"Did you find anything?" Stella asked.

"She called the arts school multiple times. Twice on Monday afternoon."

"That's highly incriminating," Stella said, feeling cold shivers run down her spine.

"I called the school as soon as I saw those records. The receptionist can't remember that conversation in particular, and said the afternoon was very busy, but she admitted that she did give out Isabella's home address to a caller. She can't remember the exact reason they gave but she assumed it was for innocent purposes. She said it wasn't unusual, and that Isabella did receive deliveries regularly at her home address, and was happy for it to be given out. Of course, she blames herself now."

"Oh, poor woman. She mustn't blame herself," Stella said, angry at the stress and trauma that others now had to endure.

"So, we need to question Nicole further about her alibi and movements, and what she said in the calls. Let's wrap this up in as much detail as possible. The idea is to present a solid case, no weaknesses, zero loopholes. A full confession would be first prize."

"It would be," Stella agreed. After her traumatic confrontation with Nicole, she hoped for the support of Roth and Maxwell during the questioning, but to her dismay, Roth had other ideas.

"You were very successful in getting her to open up earlier. I'd like you to go in first. I suggest you be tough on her. After what played out at her house, she will know she's in trouble. We need to work on her fears and present her with the overwhelming evidence we already possess."

Stella knew she should feel complimented that Roth was entrusting her with this important task. Closing this case was the priority.

"I will do my best," she said.

Wrapped in worried thoughts, she stood up and walked out of the office.

How was she going to handle another session with this madwoman, without falling apart herself?

To her dismay, she met Carrie in the corridor, heading the opposite way. She hadn't seen her in the lobby when she'd arrived, but it seemed she'd simply gone to get more paperwork to tackle, because she was carrying another batch of files.

"Afternoon," Stella said politely. She wasn't going to mention the case, she decided. Carrie would perceive any talk of it to be gloating.

Stella didn't want to gloat. She didn't want to do anything to worsen the enmity Carrie harbored toward her. How Stella wished it could just disappear.

But Carrie seemed eager to discuss it. Although, as Stella discovered, her knowledge was not up to date.

"I hear you've been spinning your wheels on this case, Stella Fall," she said conversationally, heading into the lobby and dropping the files onto the desk. They landed with a resounding bang.

"Who told you that?" Stella asked cautiously, wondering where this conversation was heading.

"I've spoken to a few people who've been very confused by the lack of progress. You know, it's a strange thing, but it doesn't take much for people to start suspecting that there might be something irregular going on," Carrie then said conversationally.

Stella felt rage gather inside her, as dark and ominous as storm clouds.

"What exactly do you mean by that?" she asked.

"I'm just passing on what I heard. But I picked up there's been some talk of corruption," Carrie smiled. "Gordon Marshall is a very well respected man. His opinion is very influential. I wonder why he suspects this."

Stella felt herself crack. Suddenly, she understood Nicole's reaction a whole lot better. There were times when you got pushed past the tipping point and you stopped playing games, and instead, let rip with your true feelings.

She stepped forward, and whatever was in her face made Carrie take a hasty step back.

"Gordon Marshall is currently fighting charges of corruption himself. The accusations are valid. I should know. I was living with the family at the time. In fact, I was the one who uncovered them and told the police. It's no surprise to me at all that he should try to paint others with the same brush. That's what he does. The surprise is that you chose to believe it. Why?" she spat at Carrie.

"I didn't say –" Carrie started, but Stella interrupted.

"Because he's ultra-wealthy? If you think all ultra-wealthy and influential people are always blameless and always right, then perhaps being an FBI agent is the wrong career for you."

"I – er –" Carrie began, looking flustered, but again Stella didn't let her speak further.

"I'll tell you what else surprises me. It astounds me that an FBI agent would deliberately try to defame a colleague and spread malicious and untruthful rumors, out of pure jealousy."

There it was, that word again. It cut like a knife into Stella's mind as she said it.

Jealousy. What a destructive emotion it was.

"If I hear any more of these rumors, I'm going to trace them back to their source. And I am going to find out what that source is. I am more than capable of doing so, and you'd be surprised how people will change their thinking when they realize someone is deliberately setting out on a smear campaign," she added threateningly.

"There's really no need for that," Carrie said hastily.

"I am one hundred percent entitled to clear my name if people are spreading false facts. So be very, very careful about saying things you shouldn't. You have no idea how badly it might end for you. Right now all you can think of is getting petty victories over me, just because I happen to be working in New Haven and you'd rather be the only new agent here."

Carrie's face was a picture. Her mouth was open, but no words were coming out. Stella wasn't sure if she was even breathing at that moment.

Angrily, she pressed on. "What a small-minded attitude, Carrie Potts! You are trying to bring me down but ultimately, anything you say will backfire badly. This isn't a local college club. This is the FBI. Agents are supposed to have each other's backs, and protect the reputation of the whole organization. People are not going to have patience with petty point scoring and malicious attempts to defame. I know I'm all done with it. And now, if you'll excuse me, I have a murder suspect to interrogate, and a case to close."

Carrie looked utterly shocked, and had turned much paler than Stella recalled she'd been at the start of their little conversation. Since she clearly couldn't come up with anything coherent in response, Stella turned and marched out of the lobby.

Inside, she was seething with anger.

How she wanted to take this vendetta further. To destroy Carrie just the way that Carrie was trying to destroy her. To nullify the threat to her career.

But she couldn't. She wasn't that person.

They were both strong, intelligent women in a male-dominated environment, with unique talents and insights.

And, damn it, they both deserved to succeed, and could do so far better if they did it together and supported each other. What a shame it could never be that way, and she'd always have to deal with the claws of Carrie's rivalry, lacerating her and pulling her back.

Stella suspected that deep down, Carrie really was a toxic person. There was no law saying that toxic people couldn't be talented in other ways and ambitious to join the FBI. She was sure she'd bump up against a few of them in her career, and this just happened to be the first time.

At any rate, she'd had her say and hoped Carrie would back down, at least for a while.

Now it was time to focus on the most important issue, and the one that seriously could affect her career future.

As she walked in trepidation to the interview room door, she wondered what it would take to extract the all-important confession from Nicole. She was likely to resist. But this was her test. It was the final step in the process that would see the killer incarcerated. This was the end point to the journey that would vindicate her in Larry Hartford's eyes, and nullify the vicious rumors that Gordon Marshall was spreading.

Stella paused outside the door, taking a moment to calm her nerves.

She needed to come across as tough, uncompromising, and remain steady in the face of whatever Nicole said or did. She needed to cut through the lies and the ranting, the screaming and accusations, and wall herself off from them.

She had to be ready for a verbal attack as soon as she walked through the door, even though she knew that following her earlier behavior, Nicole would be handcuffed.

Stella imagined herself putting on a persona, as if it was a gown she was wrapping around herself. Stern, calm, uncompromising, immune to screams and threats, to shrieks and histrionics. She needed to filter out the madness and pierce through to the truth that was hiding behind.

Holding her calmness around her like a shield, prepared for anything, Stella opened the door and stepped inside.

CHAPTER TWENTY NINE

Shock resonated through Stella as she stared at the woman sitting behind the table, her hands locked behind her.

Nicole looked small and deflated. Her face was pale and drawn, her cheeks wet and streaked with tears, her eyes red and swollen.

There was no fight in her. No aggression at all. It was as if the earlier madness had been a dream. She raised her head and met Stella's eyes, staring at her for long, desperate moments.

"Help me," she whispered.

Her demeanor, and the words, knocked the breath out of Stella. She felt her defenses shatter around her. This woman was not okay.

She couldn't match up the vulnerability she saw now, with what had happened earlier. It didn't make sense at all. She felt totally confused.

Even though she had been briefed to show forcefulness, she couldn't do it. She couldn't do anything that would further damage this already broken woman, who was clearly no longer a physical threat. Instead, she needed to be gentle, and make things more comfortable for her, while they walked the difficult path of exploring the details of the crime.

Going straight around to the back of the chair, she took the handcuff key from the high shelf. She unlocked Nicole's hands. Then she passed her the box of Kleenex on the shelf.

Nicole drew her hands in front of her slowly, as if her muscles were sore. The cuffs had bitten into her wrists, leaving deep gouges in the skin. She stared down at them looking upset and confused.

Then she grasped a Kleenex and unsteadily wiped her face.

When she'd done that, Stella poured her some water.

"Thank you," Nicole whispered, her voice ragged.

"Are you all right? How are you feeling?" Stella asked.

This wasn't the way this interview was supposed to go, but she couldn't approach it any other way. This woman was in pieces. She saw it and sensed it and had to show compassion.

Tears prickled in Nicole's hazel eyes.

"I'm not well. Not well at all," she said.

"Why do you say that?" Stella asked softly.

"I – I feel I've really messed up. Big time." Nicole paused. Tears welled from her eyes. "I - I've done terrible things. Terrible. I can't go back from them." Her voice was hesitant and jerky. After the screaming earlier, she sounded hoarse, as if speech was painful.

"Can I rest?" she entreated. "Please, I need to rest."

"In a few minutes you can. Can we speak quickly first?" Stella asked.

Nicole thought about this. It was as if she was mustering her strength.

"Okay," she agreed, in a flat, quiet voice.

At least this confession was going to be simple, Stella thought. She could gently draw the information out of Nicole and there would be no need for any pressure or bullying.

"Tell me how this all started," Stella said.

"It started when I saw them together. When I saw her," Nicole grimaced, but this time it looked more like regret than anger.

"Tell me again how that made you feel?"

"It made me feel so small. Like I could never be the person she was. I felt so furious. Like, like she'd stolen something important from me."

"It must have been a very painful moment. What time of day was it?"

"It was early evening. About quarter to six. The sun was starting to set on that beach road. It was dark enough outside that Trevor had turned on a big standard lamp in the lounge, and her hair shone in the light."

Stella was pleased by the vivid recall that Nicole was offering so far.

"Then you looked in her car?"

"Yes, I was in tears. I felt so undone. Like everything I had been working for and striving for had collapsed. But at the same time, I already knew what I had to do."

"You did?" This wasn't an easy story to listen to. Stella was dreading what she would have to go through with Nicole.

"Yes. I went home. I was crying really badly; I could hardly drive. I remember thinking how lucky it was that I lived fairly close, so I didn't have too far to go."

"And when you got home?"

"I spent some time crying on my bed. And then, an hour or two later, I got up and I researched the school. I researched her. I found out who she was and I couldn't believe that she was this ex-model and that she was married! I was absolutely shocked by that. I mean, married? I had thought that she was committed to Trevor. But she was just messing around with him."

"That must have been a terrible time for you," Stella sympathized.

"I checked a lot of places to make sure she was married. I even looked up her husband. He's a really top businessman. A billionaire. There were social photos of them together and you could see they were a really high profile couple. And so that's where I had the idea. I knew it would be difficult to do. I booked some time off work so that it wouldn't interfere with my job."

The idea. Stella's heart was accelerating now.

"What did you need to do for your idea?" Stella asked quietly.

"I needed her contact details, obviously," Nicole said.

"Contact details?"

"Yes. I had to speak to her personally, so I found those out."

"So is that why you called the modeling school on Monday? What information did you obtain from that call?"

Stella waited for Nicole to say she'd gotten her home address from the receptionist.

But instead, Nicole looked confused.

"I didn't need any information. I needed to speak to Isabella personally. But the first time she wasn't there and the second time she was on another call. I waited for a while on hold, and I started feeling so nervous I realized I couldn't speak, so I hung up. I planned to try again the next day."

This was off-script and Stella didn't know why it had suddenly veered in that direction. She was starting to feel concerned. Was she handling this interview wrong? Had it been a mistake to approach her gently? Self-blame descended pitilessly. Roth would be furious if she messed this up, with such a stack of evidence available to pressure Nicole.

"What was your purpose in speaking to her?" she asked, hoping for more clarity and to get the dialogue back on track.

Nicole sighed. "This is hard to say."

She looked a wreck. Despite the wobble in the questioning, Stella could see that the pressure was tearing her apart.

"The best decision you can make now is to cooperate fully by telling everything you know," she encouraged. "Anything else is only going to cause worse trouble."

"I was going to blackmail her, of course. I was going to tell her to get her hands off of him. I was going to send her the pictures I'd taken of her car outside his place and say that I'd seen them together. I was going to threaten her that she needed to drop him, now, or else I was going to tell her husband about her affair. But then, I didn't get hold of her on Monday. And on Tuesday, she wasn't at the school at all. And then, today, you arrived," Nicole choked on the words.

Now Stella felt as if the rug had been ripped from underneath her.

Nicole hadn't ever intended to confess to the killing at all. She was confessing to the intent of something else. Worst of all, Stella couldn't hear a false note in her voice as she continued.

"I was so stressed about calling her. I felt like this was my only chance, even though it was wrong. I hated her so much. I thought even if it doesn't work, at least it might make her think twice about cheating. And then, I got so worked up that I forgot to take my meds. Which turned everything into a total disaster." Nicole swallowed hard.

Stella didn't think this interview could get any worse, but that had just been achieved. She'd gone in here to wrap up what had been a slam-dunk case, and it was falling apart in her hands.

Meds! No wonder she'd sensed something was seriously awry with Nicole.

"Can you explain about your meds?"

"I was diagnosed with depression a few years ago. It was triggered when Trevor left but there were other underlying causes as well. I went through a very bad time until I finally realized I needed to get help before I harmed myself. So I was put onto a cocktail of meds that got me back into balance. I mean, I felt normal again. I could work. I could function."

"And you've taken them since then?"

"They made a massive difference. It's been like night and day. Being on the meds allowed me to lose weight and get healthy, as well. Overeating was part of my depressive cycle."

"Write down the names of the meds for me, and the name of the prescribing psychiatrist. And where you picked up your last batch," Stella said firmly.

She waited while Nicole scribbled on the notepad with a shaking hand.

"They're in my bathroom cabinet at home if you want to check the packaging," Nicole continued anxiously.

"Have you been off them before?" Stella then asked.

"Yes. I skipped two days a while after starting them when I had stomach flu and couldn't keep anything down. The same thing happened. You see, when I stop them abruptly, I now have rebound symptoms that cause psychotic episodes. And that's what happened earlier, in the house, when you were there." Now, tears streamed down her face. "So the damage is done. I screamed out such crazy stuff, I don't know what it was, but I know it has landed me in big trouble. Also, I think I might have struck you. Did I strike you?"

Stella nodded.

"I'm sorry. Not that it means anything now. Just like that, I've gone and ruined my life. I can't believe this! I spent so much time building myself up again. I'll probably lose my job, and it's a wonderful job. Right now is the happiest I've ever been. I don't know why I didn't realize that. All I could think of was my obsession with Trevor. How damned ridiculous."

She buried her face in her hands.

"This is such a nightmare. It's what the psychiatrist warned me about. That's why she said I should always, always take my meds. Please tell me there's somehow a way out of this?"

Nicole's eyes were filled with tears.

"The evidence against you is extremely strong," Stella said.

"I know. I know. I only realized she was murdered when you arrested me and started listing the charges. I had no idea what had happened. When I called the school on Tuesday, they didn't say. But I guess you don't believe me."

Never had Stella thought that this mountain of evidence could crumble. But now, she was filled with doubts.

Would Isabella have let a clearly aggressive and unbalanced stranger into her home? And, if Nicole had killed Isabella on Tuesday morning, there would have been no reason to call the model school later on Tuesday and ask for her. Why would she have done that?

But to Stella's dismay, the devil on her shoulder was whispering in her ear that none of this mattered. That she was choosing to take this too emotionally and was approaching it in an irrational way. That the evidence was still overwhelming and the details she had just extracted were largely irrelevant.

After all, Nicole was very likely lying in a last-ditch attempt to save herself. She could have arrived at Isabella's home intending to reveal what she knew, and then had a psychotic episode once she'd been let in. The additional phone call to the model school could have been the result of a memory gap. The psychological problems she had so clearly displayed could account for every irregularity in the case.

Stella knew that if she wanted to redeem herself and her career, she should hand over to Roth and Maxwell right now. She should say she had obtained important proof that Nicole was mentally unstable, which would add more weight to the case, but would also allow the judge to mitigate the sentence which would be a compassionate outcome for the troubled woman.

There was still enough evidence to wrap this up and take Nicole down.

But, as she stared at Nicole, she saw herself in her eyes.

After her ex had been murdered, Stella had been stressed to a breaking point, traumatized, out of her depth, and emotionally battered in every way. She remembered with a twist of her stomach the sense of helplessness she'd felt, and how she'd feared that the burden of evidence would far outweigh her attempts to prove her own innocence.

Nicole was in a similar situation. Stella could feel her despair. Her vulnerability.

There was no way she could go ahead with the sensible decision for her professional future. Faced with this paradox, she felt as undone as the woman slumped opposite her.

In fact, she couldn't face her any longer. Not when she felt overwhelmed by a surge of emotion.

"Excuse me," she said.

She stood up and walked as calmly as she could out of the interview room.

Outside, she doubled over, cupping her face in her hands, sobbing out the residual grief and anguish and fear that still lurked inside her, that would always be there, because the scars of what she'd been through were so deep that time could never erase them.

The case had fallen apart, and now she felt as if she was doing the same.

Stella had no idea how she could fix this disaster.

CHAPTER THIRTY

In the darkness of her cupped hands, as Stella tried to fight off her despair and anguish, she heard a worried voice from behind her.

"You okay?"

Hastily, she spun around, scrubbing at her eyes as Maxwell approached. She felt instantly ashamed. She didn't want her team to know how vulnerable she was, that she carried scars, that she could be reduced to tears when interviewing a suspect.

It was all weakness, and Stella knew how people reacted to weakness. She'd spent a large part of her childhood and teenage years finding that out from her mother in the most brutal way.

Above all, she had no idea how to explain to a professional colleague the predicament she was in now. It was a clear choice. Let Nicole go down, or else the case fell apart. It just so happened that this choice was destroying her.

She was expecting Maxwell to be scornful of her tears, or else laugh at her. But instead, concern tautened his face.

"You're not okay. What's gone wrong? I haven't gotten to the observation room yet, I had to take an urgent call in the office. How can I help?"

That kindness made her want to start sobbing again, but now was not the time. With an iron effort at self-control, Stella blinked her tears away and forced herself to breathe deeply.

"Sorry about that. The interview's gone completely off track, and it started giving me flashbacks," she explained, feeling desperately ashamed.

"You want to talk about it?" he asked.

"No! I don't. I can't," Stella retorted, instantly raising her defenses. She couldn't allow herself to stay vulnerable. There were good reasons why she trusted nobody with her inner feelings.

"What is it? She hasn't confessed to everything?" Maxwell asked. "You want me to take a turn? New face, new approach. Remember, there's enough evidence regardless. We just need details to strengthen the case further."

Stella shook her head and then came out with the bombshell.

"I know there's enough evidence. She could go down for it." Stella thought about the mountain of proof piled up against Nicole. The days off from work, her spoken intent to kill, the fact she'd witnessed her having a psychotic break. If only it hadn't crumbled to nothing during the interview. "Maxwell, after speaking to her, I'm absolutely sure she is not the killer."

Maxwell stared at her dubiously.

"Are you one hundred percent convinced? I mean, Roth's busy organizing a press conference. Last I heard, he was on the phone with the governor telling him that we had this wrapped up and were going to make an announcement in the next few hours."

A lead weight settled in her gut. This truly was a worst-case scenario. It would be a disastrous outcome both for the FBI and also for her personally.

"I wish I wasn't. But I am one hundred percent sure," Stella said.

"Not that I'm doubting you, but I've been in these situations before and when there's this much pressure, you want it all to be perfect. When it's not perfect, it feels like it's falling apart. But it may not be. It may just be one loose end. It's normal, I promise."

He stared at her and she saw appeal in his eyes as well as hope.

"This is not normal," she insisted miserably.

Inexperienced as she was, she couldn't pretend something was fine when she knew it wasn't. But she was sure that as the more experienced partner, Maxwell would shrug off her doubts.

She waited for him to come back with a counterargument, but to Stella's surprise, even at this critical moment, his logic prevailed.

"Come with me. Let's talk this through," he said. "Tell me the problem areas, and we'll re-look at the entire scenario. There may still be something we have missed."

He hustled down the corridor with Stella close behind. Detouring into the main office to grab his laptop, Maxwell then opened the door of another interview room. Quickly, he closed it behind him.

"What's the main issue?" he asked.

"Nicole freely confessed that she had something planned, but it wasn't murder. It was blackmail. She was obsessed with the idea of getting back together with Trevor. When she saw him with Isabella, she decided to blackmail her in order to force her to break it off."

Maxwell's eyebrows shot up. "That's it?"

"That's it. But she was on strong antidepressant meds, which she's been taking for years, and she was so stressed about all of this that she skipped a few doses. That's why she ended up having a psychotic episode and trying to attack me, and screaming out all of those threats."

"She could have killed Isabella during a psychotic episode," Maxwell insisted.

"I know. She could have. But in that case, why would Isabella have let her in?"

"Perhaps she had managed to get hold of her with the blackmail demand, and Isabella let her in to discuss the situation."

Stella stared at him in frustration. He shrugged.

"I'm just looking at things the same way the jury will look at them," he said. "To be honest, I see your point. But it's a gray area. She will more than likely be found guilty after what she said and what played out."

Horror filled Stella at the thought.

"I can't let that happen," she said, thinking again of the situation she herself had been in.

"Look, your argument makes sense. And a wrongful arrest is not something we need down the line, if she does end up being cleared of the crime. The problem is that we don't have time," Maxwell reiterated. He sighed, checking his watch. "We really don't have time. But let's take a few minutes. Have another look at what we've got. Perhaps there's a gap, something that we can explore."

He opened the laptop and he and Stella leaned over it. Their shoulders brushed as they both stared down.

Everything was here on the screen. Maxwell had neatly created spreadsheets, flow charts and timelines.

"Let's start with what it can't be. What we've ruled out," he began.

"We've ruled out Larry himself. Everyone working at the house is cleared."

"We've ruled out Trevor. He has a confirmed alibi. The three clients who left Spirit Spin are cleared," Maxwell said.

"It's not anyone from Isabella's past, and I don't believe it's anyone from Trevor's past," Stella said firmly.

"So, what does that leave us with? It leaves us with the others from the spin class, who all seem to adore Trevor and be willing to forgive or ignore whatever he does," Maxwell said, with a frown.

"The motive comes back to jealousy. I strongly feel that there's no other reason. And what would trigger jealousy?" Stella asked. "It has to be connected with the affair between Isabella and Trevor. The timeline indicates it. That flared, it peaked, and then it ended. But before it ended, it sparked off a reaction that killed her."

"The affair ended on Saturday. She was killed two days later."

"Things reached boiling point on Saturday. She behaved recklessly in the studio. He called it off as a result," Stella said. "Tuesday, she was killed. Logically, what have we ignored in our reasoning?"

Maxwell stared at her thoughtfully.

"You're thinking along my lines. So I'm going to think along your lines. Let's define jealousy. What exactly are we talking about? Maybe there's an aspect we are missing, and relooking at the core concept will give us more insight," he said.

"Okay," Stella said, encouraged by his constructive approach.

Maxwell's fingers flew over the laptop keys. His face was intent as he stared down.

"Here we go. This definition says that it's an unhappy or angry desire to have something that someone else has. And this definition says it's feeling resentment, hostility or bitterness toward someone because they have something you don't."

They stared at each other. Stella felt goose bumps prickle up and down her spine as she took in his words and realized what they meant. Maxwell's return to the core meaning of jealousy had shown to her that there was something they had overlooked.

"We've missed out on a critical suspect," she said.

"You think?" Maxwell asked.

"I can't believe I didn't see it, because I should have. All the signs were there. Now I understand who must have done it. The person who would have had a strong reason for feeling murderously jealous."

They had been minutes away from making a disastrous mistake. Now, they had only minutes to correct it before Roth made the announcement about the killer's identity.

CHAPTER THIRTY ONE

With Maxwell close behind, Stella hurried up to the door of the stately home. It was bathed in late afternoon sunshine. After the gray day, the warm light illuminated the glowing fall leaves of the chestnut tree, and shone onto the marbled porch pillars.

Stella's mind felt in overload. There was such a narrow margin between success and failure. She knew this person had to be the killer, but in this investigation, her conclusions had already been proven wrong. Isabella Hartford's death had taught her that she could make mistakes, and that she had to second-guess herself every step of the way in such a complex case.

Failure felt uncomfortably close as she rang the bell. As she waited, she clasped her hands together, realizing her fingers felt cold.

A few moments later, a young woman who looked like an au-pair opened the door.

"Afternoon, can I help?" she asked.

"Yes. Is Abigail Mills at home? We're FBI agents Maxwell and Fall," Maxwell explained.

The woman looked alarmed.

"She's at home, but they're about to leave for a charity function," she said. "Is there a problem?"

"No problem at all. We won't be long, but we need to ask some further questions regarding the recent Hartford murder. Please could you call Mrs. Mills? Where can we speak?"

"In the lounge? Will that work? Come this way."

The young woman led the way into the lounge that Stella remembered from her previous visit to the home.

She and Maxwell perched on two adjacent wingback chairs. A moment later, Abigail rushed through.

She was dressed in an evening gown – a sheer, charcoal sheath with a flared, rippling hemline that seemed to be painted onto her slender figure. Her hair was done, but her make-up not yet, and her features seemed strangely blank without it compared to the last time Stella had seen her.

However, Stella did not need the benefit of make-up to ascertain that Abigail looked furious.

"What is this about? Why didn't you call ahead? We have a charity event to attend and there's a ridiculously early start time, and Paul is a speaker there," she snapped.

"I appreciate you making the time," Stella said. "Being a murder investigation, things change from hour to hour, and we need to wrap things up as fast as possible."

With an angry sigh, Abigail perched on the sofa.

"Well, what is it?"

Stella exchanged a quick glance with Maxwell.

"Actually, we would like your husband to be here also, while we question you."

Although Maxwell spoke the words, Abigail looked daggers at Stella. In her eyes, Stella saw all the fear, fury, and hatred she'd expected.

Abigail was worried that they were going to disclose sensitive topics. Topics that she had begged Stella to keep from her husband. Stella had told her that this would remain confidential. Now, a betrayal seemed imminent.

Stella had no option but to stare stonily at the other woman. In the presence of FBI agents, Abigail couldn't refuse and would be forced to comply.

Clenching her teeth, she stood up.

"Deena!" she yelled.

In a moment, the au-pair's apprehensive face appeared at the door.

"These people want Paul to join us," Abigail snapped.

Stella realized that she didn't, in fact, look angry anymore. That emotion had passed, and what remained was a deep, visceral terror. Abigail swallowed. Her gaze darted between the agents. Her breathing was rapid and Stella could see the rise and fall of her chest in that glimmering sheath of a gown.

"I'll call him," Deena said.

She darted away and in the sudden silence, the receding patter of her footsteps could be heard.

Then, a minute later, two sets of steps were audible and a tall man walked into the lounge.

He, too, was in the process of getting ready. He wore smart black pants, ironed to perfection, and a starched white shirt that fitted his broad-shouldered frame well. His brown hair was perfectly cut. At this point he, too, looked angry, but Stella thought that the petulant set to the full mouth on his otherwise handsome face might be there even when he wasn't in a foul mood.

"Evening, agents. I'm Paul Mills. Has my wife explained we're in a rush?"

"Please, sit," Stella said.

He didn't want to sit. He lowered himself reluctantly down next to his wife. Stella noted her body language. Her shoulders hunched. She seemed to shrink away from him.

"I'm grateful for you making the time," Stella then said. "We need to confirm a few details as we conclude the investigation."

"You're wrapping it up? That's great," Paul said. "I heard talk that a suspect was arrested."

"Correct. We are questioning a suspect. Mr. Mills, I would like to confirm that you went to the Spirit Spin premises this past Saturday morning?" Maxwell asked the question smoothly, in a non-aggressive tone.

Stella waited expectantly, feeling barely able to breathe as he embarked on the line of questioning that would make or break the case.

"That's correct," Paul said. "I was in the area, and my wife wanted me to fetch her jacket from the locker."

"I believe you saw the owner in a compromising position with one of his clients?" Maxwell then pressed.

"That's right," Paul's chin now jutted angrily. "I saw him screwing around with Isabella Hartford."

"Are you certain that you saw him with Isabella?" Stella asked.

Paul's tone carried somewhat less respect as he answered her question.

"Of course I'm sure. I'm not stupid or blind, and they were making out like they were in a private room."

"So you saw her clearly?"

"Yes, and I recognized her immediately. I've met her personally at charity functions in the past, and also seen her a few times when I dropped our daughter at the arts school."

"What was your opinion of Isabella's marriage after you saw them together?" Stella then asked.

Paul looked briefly surprised by the question. "I hadn't really thought about their marriage. Just about her behavior," he said.

That was a telling statement.

Stella took a deep breath. It was time to light the fuse.

"Did you ever have any thoughts about your own marriage?" she asked.

There was a brief, stunned pause.

"What do you mean by that?" Paul shouted, his tone enraged. He swung around to face Abigail. Her face now sheet white, she looked petrified. She glanced at him, and then back at Stella, as if she simply couldn't believe the extent of the agents' betrayal.

"I mean that Trevor had an unfortunate tendency to seduce his clients. Including your wife. That's why she stopped going to the spin classes, and why she asked you to fetch her jacket," Stella said.

"What the hell?" Paul thundered. Abigail was cringing away from him. His rage was a palpable force. "Is this true?"

"Of course it's not true," Abigail whispered. "Please, don't believe them. They're trying to trap me."

Stella interrupted her pleas.

"We're not trying to trap your wife, Mr. Mills. We're simply observing the irony that she actually had an affair, whereas you never got the moment you wanted."

Now the tension in the room reached snapping point. Paul sprang to his feet.

"What do you mean by that? What the hell are you implying?"

His face was purple with rage. Abigail, on the other hand, was cowering in a corner of the couch. She looked as if she was about to pass out with stress and fear.

"You're a jealous man, Paul. Your wife told us so. And there's a reason for that. Like so many jealous men, you were worried she would behave the same way you did. You were the cheater in the relationship all along. You projected your behavior onto your wife," Stella accused him.

As an experienced cheater himself, Trevor must have quickly picked up from Abigail's words and actions, that her husband's reaction would spell big trouble if he ever found them out. Stella guessed that was why he'd broken things off with her so fast.

"This is an absolute lie. You're smearing my name," Paul raged.

As Paul shouted the words, Stella thought back to the moment she'd realized what had played out.

Abigail had told her about Paul's character during their first interview, when she'd mentioned that he'd approved of the spin class being attended only by women. At that point, Stella hadn't made the logical leap that he was a jealous, controlling person, who like so many of his type, had different rules and double standards for himself.

It was when Maxwell had read out the definition of jealousy that the puzzle pieces had slotted together in her mind.

Paul was the only person who had the means, the motive, and the opportunity to murder Isabella, and now Stella was going to explain to him exactly why.

"You were upset not because you saw Isabella with Trevor, but because you couldn't have her," Stella continued. "I'm sure you had already tried. I'm sure you propositioned her on one or more of the occasions you met. Because, like so many men, you lusted after Isabella Hartford. She was a gorgeous ex-model and there was something about her that was irresistible to men. Her husband said as much. She was used to saying no to people who tried to take advantage. But when you saw her with Trevor, you realized this was your chance to force her to say yes."

"This is absolutely ridiculous. I'm calling my lawyer right now." Paul fumed, climbing to his feet.

"Just one moment," Maxwell's voice was sharp and authoritative. "Before you make any calls, please tell us your whereabouts on Tuesday morning, between seven-thirty and nine a.m."

Paul looked deeply thoughtful for a moment. The lines of tension in his face drew tighter.

"I was at work," he said. "Where else would I be?"

"Can you prove that? Or if you wait, we can check up. You own Health Emporium and their head office is in New Haven. I guess they will know if you were there, seeing as you're the boss. Your staff can easily confirm it. Perhaps you have cameras in the parking lot, with the big warehouse there, and all," Maxwell reminded him.

Now Paul was showing signs of extreme tension, wringing his hands together.

"Wait. Tuesday? I wasn't in the office. I had to go to meetings."

"Which meetings? With whom?" Maxwell pushed.

Now, finally, Abigail spoke, her words shrill and breathy.

"Tuesday morning, you left early. You were out of the house by quarter to eight, Paul, just before I left to take the children to school. I noticed how well dressed you were. I asked if you were going to a meeting and you said you were heading to the office for an important meeting. To the office," she repeated, her voice trembling. "That's what you said."

Stella and Maxwell exchanged a glance.

Now Paul turned on Abigail, looking furious.

"I said no such thing!" he blustered. "You're misremembering. Do you realize your own bad recall could land me in serious trouble? Or wait, I've realized your plan. You're doing this deliberately, aren't you, because I now know you're a cheater!"

"Were you at Isabella's house? Did you murder her?" Abigail whispered.

Paul stared at her in smoldering silence, which Stella eventually broke.

"It's likely that you called the model school's offices on Monday and asked for Isabella's home address. That's why the receptionist remembered a request. As a parent with a child in her class, and with your charity connections, you would have found it easy to give a valid reason. My theory is that you went there Tuesday morning."

Stella turned to Isabella. "What car does Paul drive, by the way?"

"He-he drives a Volvo SUV."

"Color?"

"Burgundy," she murmured, as if she felt guilty disclosing this small detail.

"Interesting," Maxwell said meaningfully, and Stella knew he was remembering the mention of the red car that Isabella's neighbor had seen.

Stella continued. "You knew you had nothing to fear in that neighborhood, and nobody would look twice at you. A wealthy man in a good car, who had a connection with Isabella. A fine, upstanding citizen, simply dropping by on an errand. Even if the staff were home they would think you'd arrived for a quick meeting or to pick up something your daughter needed for model class. Isabella knew you, and let you in. You told her what you knew, expecting her to capitulate, much as your wife is used to doing. But she didn't. She refused your proposal, told you she wasn't interested and didn't care and to get the hell out, and then things went badly wrong between you."

"How can you say such a thing?" Paul turned to Stella and she had to stop herself from flinching as she saw, for a moment, the violent threat in his posture.

Paul's mask had slipped. He'd been on the point of physically attacking her. But then, control had prevailed.

"Paul!" Abigail gasped. She had tears in her eyes. "This –you – is it true? It sounds true! Please tell them it's not!"

She sounded terrified, confirming Stella's theory that the violent streak in Paul was close to the surface.

She wished she'd picked up earlier that Paul was such an emotional abuser. He was a man who kept his wife under his dominant control, suspicious of her movements, while deliberately seeking exactly the type of involvement he accused her of.

Now, he'd gotten a lid on his anger and spoke in an even voice again.

"I won't go to jail," he addressed Abigail. "These guys don't have enough evidence. This is simply a theory they've come up with, and it's a flimsy one. I have the best legal team, on speed dial, who can easily rebut that theory. Despite your betrayal," he added. "I built a successful business. I employ hundreds of people. I'm the family breadwinner. You haven't earned a salary since we were married, and you get regularly counseled by your shrink for anxiety. Even if I'm arrested, I'll get bail, and my lawyers will do their job, and in a couple of weeks this will all be over. For me, at any rate," he added meaningfully.

"It wasn't my fault. I've always tried to support you. I can't help being anxious. And you're the one who forced me to spend time working on my appearance, rather than holding down a job," Abigail pleaded, sounding borderline hysterical.

"Support? What a joke. You've done the opposite, and you will regret this, you slut!" Paul promised her in a low, hissing voice.

She felt cold inside. She had never heard a threat uttered with such raw viciousness.

At that moment, she knew that Abigail's life was in danger. Paul blamed her for his predicament. He had killed once, and could kill again.

Worse still, what he said about a flimsy case might be proven true. They didn't have a confession from him so far, and at this point it seemed unlikely they would obtain one. If Paul was holding out for his lawyers to save him, he might take refuge in stubborn denial. Even if he was arrested, he might be able to negotiate bail, especially with his breadwinner and business owner status.

Stella didn't want to visualize the brutal scene that would play out in this home when Paul arrived back.

Panic descended. She'd believed her theory was rock-solid. Now, she saw its weaknesses. It might fail, and as a result, another innocent woman could die.

Was there a way to turn around this potentially catastrophic situation, Stella wondered frantically.

Suddenly, she thought of a solution that might work.

CHAPTER THIRTY TWO

Stella knew, in that moment, what she needed to do. She'd gotten the hint in Paul's body language, that frightening instant where he'd tensed, about to turn on her. She had to tap into that murderous streak again. Dangerous as it might be, she had to force Paul to attack her.

A physical assault on an FBI agent, in front of witnesses, would convince any court to deny bail and keep Paul in jail. Also, it would strengthen the murder case against him.

How could she do that? How could she pressure him to violence?

She needed to take him back to that confrontation with Isabella again, because that was the moment where his control had slipped. Then, she needed to push for the explosion.

Jealousy most commonly stemmed from insecurity, Stella reminded herself. Deep down, Paul was vastly insecure. His veneer of confidence concealed a toxic abyss of self-doubt and self-hatred. She needed to smash that layer and plunge into his depths.

Stella stood up and stepped squarely in front of Paul. She put her hands on her hips and raised her chin. He drew himself together defensively at her show of confidence and strength. No wonder poor Abigail had learned such passive behavior, she thought briefly, as she started speaking.

"Let's cut to the chase about what really happened, shall we, Paul?" she said in dismissive tones. "You're a jealous man. And you were insane with jealousy that Isabella would sleep with a fitness instructor and not with you, despite you pestering and badgering her in the past."

"What?" he shot back reflexively. He was bristling now, defensive and worried all over again.

"When you arrived at Isabella's house on Tuesday morning, you had what you thought was the deal-maker. You must have felt confident going into that gym where she had just started her workout. You thought that by threatening to tell Larry Hartford about her affair, you had what it would take to force her."

Her taunting words were having an effect. Paul had gone very still. She hoped adrenaline was surging inside him at the words, eroding his logic, drawing him into a flight or fight response.

Stella was going to push for the fight, even though she saw the worry clear on Maxwell's face as she deliberately inflamed the situation.

"I'm sure you got a huge thrill thinking of the power you now wielded, and how horrified she'd be when you dropped the bombshell. What a shame it didn't work out how you assumed it would. Everything went wrong, didn't it?"

Paul clamped his lips together. It was a sign he was fighting for control, Stella hoped.

"What do you think happened?" Abigail asked in a small voice.

"Isabella was tired of her marriage. She was ready to leave her husband. Probably, she laughed at Paul and said his efforts were pathetic, and that he'd be doing her a favor if he told Larry what he'd seen," Stella said firmly, and although her words were addressed to Abigail, she stared at Paul to confirm the truth of it.

"This entire conversation is a falsity," Paul said, but his voice was shaking and uncertain.

"Her rejection bludgeoned your ego and it pushed you over the edge. I'm sure there were other factors, too. Did your threats backfire on you, Paul? Did Isabella then promise to expose you, to tell your wife what you'd done, to smear your name? I'm sure she wanted to get revenge after your clumsy attempt at coercion. That would have been a rude shock. Suddenly you realized just how badly this could turn out for you."

Paul was blinking rapidly. His mouth was open, forming silent words, as if voicing a denial that only he could hear or believe.

"You acted in a red-hot rage to save yourself. You grabbed that rope and you strangled her with it. Is that true, Paul? Is that how things played out?"

"Is it true? It sounds true," Abigail echoed, her voice high and quivering.

Paul was going to break. His arms jerked toward Stella and she braced herself, readying for the attack that would follow.

But, instead of launching himself at her, Paul swung furiously toward Abigail.

"It wouldn't be true if you hadn't started this whole debacle!"

At last, this was the confession they needed, but Stella realized with a clench of her stomach that things had spiraled way out of control.

"This is your fault!" Paul ranted to his wife. "I didn't think I'd married such a slut! If you'd kept your legs closed, you wouldn't have landed me in this trouble. Of course I didn't mean to kill Isabella, but she provoked me, just like you're doing now!"

"Don't say such a thing!" Abigail screamed. Her voice was shrill with tension. Tears streamed down her face.

She did something, clumsily, with her feet. Stella didn't realize what it was until Abigail sprang up. Only then did Stella see she'd kicked off her spindly, elegant, high heeled shoes.

"Don't hurt me!" she pleaded, before fleeing from the room.

Her show of terror finally triggered the outpouring of aggression in Paul. Roaring with anger, he stormed after her. "I'm going to kill you, bitch! But first, I'm going to hurt you so bad you'll regret every moment you lived."

"We have to contain this," Maxwell shouted, racing out of the lounge in pursuit. "Guy's deranged."

Stella was shocked by the suddenness at which he'd flipped over from controlled fury into murderous action. She'd expected him to attack her, but like a true bully, he'd gone for the target he perceived to be the weakest.

Rushing out of the lounge in pursuit, Stella imagined how Isabella had felt when it happened to her. Paul must have changed in a flash, his violent side unchecked, his demons exposed.

Isabella had no chance at all and must have died in terror.

Abigail had lived with the same fear, the same inherent threat of violence. And now, it had reached the point of no return. She was shrieking in fright as she ran. She reached a doorway and dived into the room, slamming it behind her. Stella heard the frantic scrabble of the key in the door, but before she could lock it, Paul flung himself against it.

"I go down, you go down too. Forever," he roared, bursting through the doorway.

The door crashed shut again. The lock turned, and her screams reached a crescendo.

"Help her, help her," Stella whispered to herself as she ran.

Maxwell reached the door and grabbed it, wrestling with the handle. As Stella rushed to help him, she heard a small frightened voice behind her.

"Please, what's going on?"

The au pair, her face drawn with anxiety, was standing near the foot of the stairs, peering down the corridor.

"Go back up," Stella told her urgently, above the crashing thumps as Maxwell tried to force his way in. "Lock yourself and the kids inside somewhere, and then call the cops."

Wide-eyed, the au pair nodded. Then she turned and hurried up the elegant stairway.

Spinning back, Stella saw Maxwell jump high, delivering a roundhouse kick to the door, with all his force, at the level of the lock. The jamb splintered with a crunching noise and the ruined door flew open, revealing the sumptuously decorated spare bedroom beyond.

Rushing in behind him, Stella felt sick with horror as she saw Paul was attacking Abigail. He'd grabbed his wife with both his strong hands, forcing her down on the immaculate cream bedcovers, crushing her thin, vulnerable neck.

He could do serious damage in a few moments with his strength and that insane grip, Stella realized.

"Stop it! Let her go! You're going to kill her!" Maxwell lunged forward, grabbing at Paul's hands, wrestling with him as he tried desperately to pry his fingers away.

Paul kicked out viciously at Maxwell and almost managed to connect. Maxwell ducked away, cursing.

It was clear Paul didn't care. He had already shown he had no inhibitions about killing.

Breathing hard, his face drawn with tension, Maxwell stepped back. Stella realized that in the next moment, he had an impossible choice to make. In order to force Paul to release his death grip, he was going to have to either shoot him, or else physically assault him.

Given that Paul had turned violent beyond reason, both choices carried serious implications and risks, for Maxwell both personally and professionally, and also for Abigail.

His face taut with worry, Maxwell made the decision he thought would carry the least risk. He reached for his holster.

But maybe there was a third way, Stella thought.

"Wait!" she shouted to Maxwell.

Leaping into the fray from behind Paul, she wrapped her own hands round his neck.

Let's see how you like it, she thought, digging her fingers viciously into the flesh above his starched white collar, choking off his airway with all the force she possessed, hoping that he would react exactly the same way his victim had.

It was exactly the right move. Instinct took over, and Paul responded just as Isabella had done. His hands dropped from Abigail's neck and flew to his own throat, clawing helplessly at her grip. He coughed and retched while his body began flailing. His fingers tore at her skin.

Stella let go his neck. First priority was to save Abigail. She rushed to grab her under her arms and drag her out of reach. Abigail was hysterical, gagging, but she was at least alive and her husband's attack had not caused irreparable damage.

Her chokehold had paid off. Paul was still wheezing and coughing, doubled over as he fought to get air back into in his lungs. While he struggled to breathe, she and Maxwell managed to wrestle his hands behind him and snap the cuffs securely in place.

"You're under arrest," Maxwell told him, breathlessly. "Paul Mills, we are arresting you on suspicion of the murder of Isabella Hartford."

Stella felt a rush of relief and vindication as they manhandled the now sobbing man to his feet. Finally, and without a doubt, their hunt for the killer was over.

CHAPTER THIRTY THREE

It was dark by the time Stella arrived back at the New Haven FBI office. Paul's arrest had been processed at the local precinct. Roth had been so busy she'd barely seen him. He'd been dealing with the paperwork, finalizing the details, organizing a press conference, and having a second emergency meeting with the governor.

After hours, this place had a different feel to it. It was quieter, more hushed, as if the beating heart of the building hadn't stopped, but had slowed. And to her relief, Carrie was no longer stationed in the lobby, where a new pile of files had arrived, Stella saw. She'd gone home and Stella hoped she'd had a chance to think about the warning she'd given her.

Of course, Stella's warning might have come too late. She still had no idea what Roth would decide. She guessed that being a man who didn't like to waste time, he would make his decision fast. Perhaps even by the time he got back to New Haven.

Which was now. Hearing rushed footsteps, she turned to face the door. She'd worked with Roth for long enough to recognize his incoming footfalls, and sure enough, a moment later, he appeared in the doorway.

"Got to get a haircut," he muttered to himself, impatiently pushing back his overgrown bangs. Then he saw her.

"Ah, Fall. Glad you're here. I wanted to speak to you."

Stella waited, barely daring to breathe. She felt paralyzed with nerves and worry. This decision was so enormous. It would literally decide her future.

"Yes, Roth," she replied politely. Her voice sounded small and scared.

"I can't emphasize enough how important it was for all of us that this case was solved quickly." He sighed, letting out a deep breath. "It was thanks to your efforts that we were able to arrest the right suspect, with a one hundred percent confirmed admission of guilt. It was down to the wire, make or break, and thanks to you, it wasn't break."

"Thank you," Stella said gratefully.

No matter what happened next, she felt on top of the world to receive Roth's praise. Even if she was forced to relocate, she would have a successful track record thanks to this case. But she hoped she wouldn't have to do that. She didn't want to move!

"Larry Hartford has asked me to convey his thanks personally. I explained to him what you'd done and how far you'd gone to solve this. He wants to organize a special event to recognize you for your determination and resourcefulness. It'll be held early in November, at one of the local hotels. He's getting a few of his stakeholders involved. It's going to create a lot of positive publicity for our department, and for you in particular," Roth said, sounding satisfied.

"Oh, that's amazing!" Stella said, unable to keep the surprise out of her voice. This was completely unexpected.

"I also spoke to the governor and explained the history you told me. He was surprised to hear it. He said the rumors hadn't come directly from Gordon Marshall or he would have taken them less seriously, knowing the legal drama that's playing out."

"I see," Stella's mouth felt dry.

"He apologized to me. He said that he was too quick to believe a one-sided story and that it was due to the family pressure of the crime. He said that he will handle any further rumors very firmly and he will make sure that he confirms everything factually from the source," Roth gave a short laugh. "He actually said this was a lesson for him in how to handle evidence."

"That's great news," Stella said. It was sounding positive, but she still didn't know what that meant for her.

"I've decided that thanks to your work on the case, and as a result of what the governor has said, we should fast-track you to a junior field agent. I think that having successfully solved such a high profile crime, we need to get you out and about. It's the right thing to do politically, with Hartford having commended you so highly, and it's also the right thing to do for my department, because we need talent and ability to be visible, and placed where it can be used most effectively."

Stella stared at Roth in amazement. What a turnaround. The rumors that Gordon Marshall had hoped would cause damage had ended up working in her favor. Her career would be fast tracked. She'd be where she had hoped and dreamed of being in a year or two – out on the streets and solving crimes.

"Thank you, Roth!" she said, unable to suppress a huge, happy smile.

"I'm glad it has worked out this way," he agreed. His tone was warmer than she'd ever heard it. "Of course, the basic work has to be done and we'll all chip in with that." He glanced at the pile of files as if wondering how on earth new ones kept materializing. "But I'm grateful to have someone so capable and determined to be fighting with us on the frontlines. There are enough of the bad guys. They seem to multiply daily, and we can all see how effective they are."

"I am so grateful that you believed me," Stella said.

Roth gave her a sideward glance. "Trust me, I did my research. A couple of detectives in Greenwich that I know personally vouched for you and confirmed your side."

Stella thought immediately of Detective Bradshaw, who'd headed up the investigation into Vaughn's murder. He was the one who'd suggested she go into law enforcement. She felt thankful beyond words that he'd spoken in her favor now.

"So. We start again tomorrow." Roth checked his watch. "Better get home, and enjoy an early night while we can. It's not often we can leave the office feeling that we've had such a win."

His rare smile lit up his face.

As Stella took the passage to the underground lot where her small and recently purchased Ford was parked, she saw Maxwell coming in.

"I wanted to find you," he explained. "Roth said he was going to speak to you about the rumors, and what he'd decided to do. I didn't know what to expect," he said.

His face was impassive, but his tone was anxious. Maxwell had also been worried about the outcome, she realized.

"It's all okay. It's ended up fine," Stella felt overwhelmed by happiness. "Roth believed my version, and he's said that I'm going to be fast-tracked and be out in the field as soon as possible."

Maxwell's eyebrows shot up.

"Boy, I'm relieved," he confided. "Roth usually makes good decisions, but there were a lot of complicating factors, and with that whole political angle, I was stressed out."

"Me, too," Stella shared.

"You want to go to dinner this evening?" he asked.

There was something in his tone, and the use of that particular word, that made her look at him more closely. She didn't quite know what level of invitation this was.

Maxwell reddened.

"Just to celebrate solving the case, and becoming an active part of the team," he added hastily. "That's what I meant. In case you were wondering. Dinner, as in, the evening meal. With a glass of wine, of course."

Stella grinned at him. Of course she'd wondered, and she appreciated that Maxwell had skillfully backpedaled to make sure this invite was on a level she could handle right now.

Dinner with Maxwell? She was looking forward to it. Not only to strengthen their working relationship but also, maybe, because the spark inside her that she felt from time to time in his presence, was fizzing at the thought.

"How about a cocktail first?" she suggested. "I can be ready in an hour. Tell me where we should meet."

*

"Oh, boy," Rebecca said, exhaling deeply as she leaned her elbows on the kitchen table. "This is a hectic story, Stella. Beyond crazy. I can't believe you've been through all of this in the past few days! No wonder you got a long weekend off," she said.

"I'm glad your company closes early on Fridays, and we could arrange this," Stella said.

"So you're going to stay overnight. As soon as Marco gets back, we'll order pizza and I'll make sangria. I have the fruit, the red wine, everything we need. But for now, I want to talk about what you just told me. I have so many questions about how you felt, and how you made your decisions. I want to hear every detail, all over again – if you're okay with it," Rebecca said.

"I'm very okay with it. It feels like therapy being able to discuss it with a friend," Stella said.

"I must say, I think you were Nicole's angel. You stepped in and made sure she was cleared and okay. I'm glad she was released without any charges being pressed. I hope she makes a success of her life now and finds someone decent to fall in love with."

"I feel exactly the same," Stella agreed. "I was so torn up about her. I couldn't bear to think she might go down for something that wasn't her fault, just because she'd made a bad relationship choice."

Rebecca shook her head. "Relationships are such volatile things. It makes me glad I'm in a stable one right now. And you?" She tilted her head, gazing at Stella questioningly. "Any signs of love on the horizon?"

"No. Not yet. But I've made some good new friends," Stella said firmly, resolving not to get ahead of herself. One dinner did not make a romance, even though it had been a wonderful few hours. She and Maxwell were working colleagues and she knew that was top of mind for him, as well as for her. Neither of them could risk emotional fallout affecting their career.

For now, she felt very grateful that he was a firm friend – with a spark.

"Well, that's promising." Rebecca tilted her head, "Is that your phone? I heard a beep."

Stella groped in her purse and found her phone.

She drew in a sharp breath. "It's from my mother!"

"That's unusual," Rebecca observed.

"You don't know how unusual. She blocked my number on Tuesday, after I pressured her to tell me the truth about my dad," Stella said.

"Oh, hell!" Rebecca sounded stressed. "I just don't know what to make of all this. I wish things could be different. She must have unblocked you, though, or you wouldn't be getting the text."

"I know." Stella looked down at her phone in trepidation. She felt as if she was staring at a poisonous snake. There were no guarantees where Rhonda Fall was concerned. Stella knew to expect the unexpected, every time and in the worst possible way.

Most likely, her mother had just decided on a few more vicious insults to fling at her. She didn't want to open this text.

"You need to read it," Rebecca encouraged. "You can't ignore it. Just take a look. It's only words. They will hurt, but I'm here. We can talk about it and it will help to make the whole ordeal less painful."

She reached over and gripped Stella's left hand, her fingers warm, as Stella navigated her phone with her right.

She opened the message. She read it.

Then she stared at it, excitement flooding through her. She hardly dared to breathe as she read and re-read the words, not understanding what they meant, but knowing that this was an important clue she now had to follow, no matter what it took.

The message consisted of one simple, short sentence.

"Last known address: 5 Wilderness Avenue, Ouray, Colorado."

Finally, Stella had a starting point. She knew where her father had gone after his disappearance, even if it was years ago.

Now, she could take the first step on the journey to find him.

NOW AVAILABLE FOR PRE-ORDER!

HIS OTHER MISTRESS

(A Stella Fall Psychological Suspense Thriller—Book 4)

When a 40-year-old mother and divorcee is found murdered after a wild college house party, FBI Special Agent Stella Fall suspects there's more to the story than partying gone awry.

HIS OTHER MISTRESS is book #4 in a new psychological suspense series by debut author Ava Strong, which begins with HIS OTHER WIFE (Book #1).

As Stella delves deeper into the case, it only becomes more complex and confusing, leading her to dead end after dead end. Stella must use her brilliant mind to unravel the questions at the heart of the case: Why was this divorcee at the party in the first place? Who wanted her dead? And why?

And will the killer strike again?

A fast-paced psychological suspense thriller with unforgettable characters and heart-pounding suspense, HIS OTHER MISTRESS is book #4 in a riveting new series that will leave you turning pages late into the night.

Future books in the series will be available soon.

Ava Strong

Debut author Ava Strong is author of the REMI LAURENT mystery series, comprising three books (and counting); of the ILSE BECK mystery series, comprising four books (and counting); and of the STELLA FALL psychological suspense thriller series, comprising four books (and counting).

An avid reader and lifelong fan of the mystery and thriller genres, Ava loves to hear from you, so please feel free to visit www.avastrongauthor.com to learn more and stay in touch.

BOOKS BY AVA STRONG

REMI LAURENT FBI SUSPENSE THRILLER
THE DEATH CODE (Book #1)
THE MURDER CODE (Book #2)
THE MALICE CODE (Book #3)

ILSE BECK FBI SUSPENSE THRILLER
NOT LIKE US (Book #1)
NOT LIKE HE SEEMED (Book #2)
NOT LIKE YESTERDAY (Book #3)
NOT LIKE THIS (Book #4)

STELLA FALL PSYCHOLOGICAL SUSPENSE THRILLER
HIS OTHER WIFE (Book #1)
HIS OTHER LIE (Book #2)
HIS OTHER SECRET (Book #3)
HIS OTHER MISTRESS (Book #4)

www.ingramcontent.com/pod-product-compliance
Lightning Source LLC
Chambersburg PA
CBHW030616310726
48979CB00003B/747